HEART OF THE CAT

SARAFIN WARRIORS BOOK 3

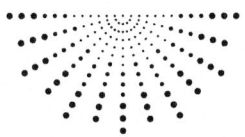

S.E. SMITH

ACKNOWLEDGMENTS

I would like to thank my husband Steve for believing in me and being proud enough of me to give me the courage to follow my dream. I would also like to give a special thank you to my sister and best friend, Linda, who not only encouraged me to write, but who also read the manuscript. Also to my other friends who believe in me: Julie, Jackie, Christel, Sally, Jolanda, Lisa, Laurelle, Debbie, and Narelle. The girls that keep me going!

And a special thanks to Paul Heitsch, David Brenin, Samantha Cook, Suzanne Elise Freeman, and PJ Ochlan—the awesome voices behind my audiobooks!

—S.E. Smith

HEART OF THE CAT: SARAFIN WARRIORS BOOK 3
Copyright © 2019 by Susan E. Smith
First E-Book Published February 2019
Cover Design by Melody Simmons
ALL RIGHTS RESERVED: This literary work may not be reproduced or transmitted in any form or by any means, including electronic or photographic reproduction, in whole or in part, without express written permission from the author.

All characters, places, and events in this book are fictitious or have been used fictitiously, and are not to be construed as real. Any resemblance to actual persons living or dead, actual events, locales, or organizations are strictly coincidental.

Summary: When Trescina get a call for help with an injured predatory cat, this 'new species' sounds enough like a shapeshifter that she hurries to take charge of the situation, and it isn't long before she discovers just how precarious the situation is. Assassins, traitors, and a Goddess with a guiding hand culminate in more than one life-threatening secret….

ISBN: (KDP Paperback) 9781796591347
ISBN: (BN Paperback) 9781078746595
ISBN: (eBook) 9781944125660

Romance (love, brief explicit sexual content) | Science Fiction (Aliens) | Action/Adventure Thriller | Royal | Contemporary | Paranormal (Shifters) | Fantasy

Published by Montana Publishing, LLC
& SE Smith of Florida Inc. www.sesmithfl.com

CONTENTS

Prologue	1
Chapter 1	13
Chapter 2	24
Chapter 3	34
Chapter 4	39
Chapter 5	55
Chapter 6	64
Chapter 7	74
Chapter 8	81
Chapter 9	89
Chapter 10	99
Chapter 11	108
Chapter 12	119
Chapter 13	130
Chapter 14	136
Chapter 15	143
Chapter 16	151
Chapter 17	160
Chapter 18	167
Chapter 19	173
Chapter 20	178
Epilogue	184
Additional Books	195
About the Author	199

CAST OF CHARACTERS

Walkyr d'Rojah

- Prince of the Sarafin royal family
- Third oldest

Trescina Bukov

- Human
- Expert on Big Cats
- Mate to Walkyr

Katarina Bukov-Danshov

- Half-sister to Trescina Bukov

Mia Elena d'Rojah-Bukov

- Daughter of Queen Mia d'Rojah and King L'Darma Bukov
- Mate to Raul T'Rivre
- Mate to Ivan Danshov
- Two daughters: Trescina Bukov (Raul) and Katarina Bukov-Danshov (Ivan)

Raul T'Rivre

- Mate to Princess Mia Elena d'Rojah-Bukov (on Sarafin)
- Biological father of Trescina Bukov
- Captain of the Guard for the King and Queen of the Forest Kingdom of Sarafin
- High Lord of the Secret Sect of *The Enlightened*

Ivan Danshov

- Human mate to Mia Elena d'Rojah-Bukov (on Earth)
- Scientist for Wildlife Conservation Society (WCS)
- Biological father of Katarina Danshov

Vox d'Rojah - King of the Sarafin

- Cat shifter
- Sarafin warrior
- Mate to Riley St. Claire

Riley St. Claire

- Mate to Vox d'Rojah
- Human

Aryeh

- Father of the Sarafin Princes

Rosario

- Mother of the Sarafin Princes

Illana

- Sister to Aryeh

Viper

- Prince of the Sarafin royal family
- Second oldest

Gable

- Prince of the Sarafin royal family
- Fourth oldest

Qadir

- Prince of the Sarafin royal family
- Fifth oldest

Pallu

- Prince of the Sarafin royal family
- Youngest of the princes
- Sixth oldest

Eldora

- Former lover of Vox d'Rojah
- Informant for those trying to overthrow the royal families
- Killed by poison

Pursia

- Former lover of Vox d'Rojah
- Informant for those trying to overthrow the royal families
- Committed suicide

Titus – Rightful Ruler of the Ocean Kingdom

- Vox's cousin
- Sarafin warrior

Banu – Rightful Ruler of the Desert Kingdom

- Sarafin warrior
- Adopted by Illana and Arimis
- Raised as Titus' younger brother

- Parents murdered in their sleep
- Illana's younger brother was his father

Lodar

- medical officer

Tor

- chief of engineering for the *Shifter* warship

Bragnar

- Sarafin warrior
- Traitor/assassin

Vladimir Mirvo

- Russian poacher/black market trader

Airabus

- Former Elite Palace guard
- Sarafin Traitor

Ranker

- Sarafin Traitor

Nastran

- Sarafin Traitor

Heather Arnold

- Vet for Grove Ranch

- Administrator of Wyoming Rescue Center
- Mother to Zeke Reynolds

Zeke Reynolds

- 11-year-old son of Heather Arnold

Terry James

- Part-time volunteer at the Wyoming Rescue Center

SYNOPSIS

Prince Walkyr d'Rojah's mission is to find an ancient artifact known as the Heart of the Cat—a powerful gem that connects his people, its magic woven through the Sarafin like his predatory cat is woven into himself. Walkyr's only clues are an ancient scroll and the legends passed down through generations. However, he isn't the only one searching for the it. A sect determined to overthrow the royal families of the Sarafin, the Curizan, and the Valdier wants the gem for themselves. They are more than willing to do whatever it takes to obtain it.

Trescina Bukov's affinity with large cats has taken her all over the world, but this time a frantic call from a rescue group compels her to fly to Wyoming in the United States. A new species of leopard was discovered near death, she's told, and this 'new species' sounds enough like a shape-shifter that Trescina hurries to examine this cat.

Their first meeting is explosive, and Walkyr is shocked when the human female connects with his leopard—recognizing what he is and what his weaknesses are, and this is only the beginning of how his mission has gone wrong! Assassins, traitors, and a Goddess with a guiding hand culminate in more than one life-threatening secret….

PROLOGUE

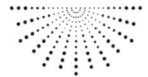

Forest Kingdom on Sarafin:
Centuries Before

Mia could see the raging fires through the open windows of the palace as she ran barefoot along the dark corridors. The brilliant flames gave the night a malevolent glow. Terrified screams rang through the air and added to the chaos and confusion.

Mia's heart thundered in her chest when she heard urgent shouts behind her. She quickly turned left and ran down another long corridor to seek a place to hide. All around her, she could hear the pleading voices of the servants begging for their lives before their cries were brutally silenced.

She stumbled as she fled down one corridor after another in a desperate search for the one place that might save her life—and the life of her unborn child. Clad only in a thin nightgown and cloak, she shivered from shock and the cold stone beneath her bare feet. Tears blinded her, and she barely stifled the grief threatening to overwhelm her.

She brushed away the tears that burned her eyes with a shaking hand. Her parents, the King and Queen of the Forest Kingdom, and the palace guards were dead, murdered by traitors. Her mate had also been murdered.

Mia's cat had awoken her with a hiss of warning, and frightened by her cat's urgency, she had fled down the corridor to her mate's study. Raul often retired there in the evenings when he couldn't sleep.

Mia almost hadn't had enough time to hide behind a large column. She'd heard them coming, their footsteps accompanied by the sound of screams, then seconds later, Mia had witnessed at least a dozen armed men stop in front of Raul's study. Most of Raul's attackers had concealed their faces, but her cat could sense that some of them were not from Sarafin.

She had turned away, her back pressed to the column and her fist pressed against her mouth. There was no way her mate could survive such an onslaught, but Mia had been unable to abandon the desperate hope that somehow they would not kill him. She peered around the column, watching one of the men standing in the doorway, his sword dripping with Raul's blood. His cloak didn't have a hood to conceal his features, and she had recognized his face all too well—Airabus. They had grown up together. Once, she had considered him a friend.

Beyond him, she could see a body in the shadows of the room. Her mate lay dead—murdered by the warrior he'd thought was his best friend and ally.

She had remained in her hiding place, trembling with the strength of her grief. As the group moved down the hallway, led by a man dressed in an elegant, black, hooded cloak edged in gold, Airabus had commented to another man that he hoped the attacks on the other Sarafin kingdoms were going as well as this one. Mia had listened intently as he talked about the simultaneous attacks against the Valdier and Curizan home worlds. He said the three ruling families would soon be completely destroyed and replaced.

She had recoiled when she heard Airabus mention Prince Raffvin, a

Royal Valdier Dragon Lord. She was stunned that any Sarafin would work with a Valdier Prince to murder the Sarafin royal family. How could they turn on their own people? When they were out of sight, she turned and fled.

It had been an hour since then, and she felt like the nightmare would never end. She heard footsteps approaching from the west wing and fruitlessly wiped at her tears as she once again squeezed as much of her body into an alcove as she could. Shifting into her cat would make her slightly more dangerous, but she was vastly outnumbered, and there were fewer possible hiding places for a tiger than there were for a woman. She held her breath as a group of warriors ran past.

There was only one person she could trust now. Mia had not spoken or seen the Goddess Aikaterina since Mia was a little girl, but she hoped that the Goddess would hear and answer her plea now.

It was not common knowledge that the very existence of the Sarafin species depended on the gift that the Goddess had given them: the power to shift into large predatory cats—and it was certainly not widely known that the power came from the blood of the royal family as much as it came from the blood of the Goddess Aikaterina. By destroying the royal family, the traitors were destroying themselves. There was only one way to prevent that—the Heart of the Cat.

I sense danger, her cat hissed. *They wait for you.*

We must get to the chamber, Mia instructed, knowing that there was no other choice. *There is another passageway. We will use it.*

The traitors may know about it, her cat warned.

Mia shook her head. *There is no way anyone else could know of the chamber. Aikaterina warned me that I must not tell anyone, including my mate. Only I know the way to the chamber,* she reminded her cat, her throat tightening with grief at the thought of her dead mate.

Shift, her cat commanded.

Mia carefully scanned the area before she shifted. Once deep inside her cat, she soothed the small cub nestled inside her. The cub sensed the danger they were in, but it was more than that—the tiny life inside of her felt the loss of her father. Grief almost paralyzed Mia as the image of her dead mate flashed through her mind. A shudder ran through the large black tiger.

Go, she ordered, pushing aside her grief.

The black tiger silently slipped back into the wide corridor. She hugged the wall away from the windows, trying to keep in the shadows as much as possible. At the end of the corridor, she lifted her head and sniffed the air. Her cat curled her lip, revealing sharp teeth. She remained silent. As much as she wanted to attack the Curizan and Valdier warriors she scented, she knew that it would be a futile endeavor that would only lead to her capture or death.

Traitors! her cat silently snarled. *They work with Curizan and Valdier— Traitors to Sarafin.*

We must protect our cub. If we are captured, they will kill her, Mia reminded her cat.

Her cat turned her head and looked up. There was a small staircase that led to a room above the chamber they sought. If they could slip into it, they could follow a hidden passage down to the chamber and then continue to their destination below the palace.

Mia's cat pulled back into the shadows and retreated several feet to a narrow spiral staircase that opened onto the balcony. Her belly hung low, at times rubbing against the worn stone steps as she climbed. Warmth filled her when she heard purring. Her daughter thought it was funny that Mia's belly was so big that it dragged against the steps.

That is because you are going to be big and strong like your father, Mia teased, trying to distract the cub from the seriousness of the situation.

Gone.

That word caused a feeling of sorrow to sweep through Mia. The cub was far enough along to understand more than Mia had realized. She winced when she felt a sharp pain cut across her abdomen. Her tiger paused and waited. Fortunately, the pain was brief.

At the top of the stairs, Mia paused and peered from her vantage point above the corridor below. The two guards had been joined by two more that were positioned to cut off anyone trying to escape. The new warriors were also Sarafin. She watched with rage as they shifted and rolled their shoulders.

"Have they found her yet?" the Valdier guard asked.

"No, but she is heavy with a cub, and the High Lord has sealed the palace. She cannot go anywhere. The night is almost over. Once the sun rises, she won't be able to hide in the shadows," Airabus stated.

"Has there been word on the other kingdoms?" the Curizan asked.

In the dim light, Mia could see Airabus grin. His sharp-toothed smile was marred by the fact that one of his canines was broken in half. Her claws dug into the wood, slicing through the long rug and leaving deep gouges. She wanted to slice his throat.

"The King of the Desert Kingdom and his mate are dead, but the young prince is missing. The others will fall soon. Lord Raffvin is working to ensure that," Airabus replied.

"It is a shame that Princess Mia never knew the truth about her mate's past. I wonder if she would still mourn him if she did," the Valdier sneered.

Mia lowered herself to the floor as a wave of confusion hit her. She waited to see if the warrior would continue, but Airabus hissed at the man to shut up. She pulled back into the shadows of the railing when Airabus looked up, as if sensing her watching.

With painful slowness, she crawled back until she was pressed against the wall. Rising partially to her feet, she moved to the end of a small decorative area. With a press of her nose, a panel opened near the bottom, and she slipped through the opening and disappeared into the hidden passage, the panel automatically sealing behind her.

Shifting, she held her stomach with one hand and the wall with the other. She carefully followed the winding maze of hidden staircases and narrow corridors until she reached the entrance to the room she was seeking. The sharp pains had returned, and she knew she was in labor.

Mia stumbled forward until she reached the end of the staircase. Ahead of her was the chamber Aikaterina had shown her when she was a child. She walked to the far wall and pulled on the lever that opened the secret door. The panel silently slid open, and Mia stepped inside. Her breathing sounded loud in the large room. She panted as she tried to control the pain from her contractions.

She gazed around the chamber. The room had a soft glow, radiating upward from a central pedestal. The light reflected off the white ceiling and walls. A pool of clear liquid surrounded the pedestal, and on top of the pedestal was an ornate basin. A series of rocks created a bridge that led to the treasure concealed in the shallow, curved basin.

Mia slowly walked around the edge of the pool, then paused and shifted again. Her tiger emitted a soft, rumbling groan as another contraction swept through her. Her stomach tightened, and she panted.

We are almost there. I cannot reach the center. Only you can, she reminded her cat.

Her cat grunted in response. Her shimmering silver eyes focused on the first step. With a graceful leap, she landed on the rock. The stepping stone moved, and she whipped her tail to steady herself.

She waited until the rock stopped moving before she jumped to the next one. With another leap, she landed on the next rock. Once again, the stone shifted. This time the movement caused a slight wave and some of the liquid splashed up onto her front paw. She quickly lifted her foot and shook it when she received a painful burn. The liquid looked like water, but it was a corrosive acid pool designed to keep the Heart of the Cat safe.

Hurt, her cat whimpered, nursing her paw against her chest.

I know. You must be careful, Mia replied.

I try. Cub coming, her cat panted.

Mia didn't respond. She focused on calming the cub. The infant was squirming in distress. She couldn't come yet. It was too dangerous. She needed to get to the center area and safety.

Placing her injured paw on the stone, she focused on her next leap. Time was running out. She heard footsteps approaching, and her fear threatened to choke her. Somehow, the High Lord had discovered the secret passage.

You must hurry. We have to get to the Heart before it is too late, Mia desperately ordered.

They smaller. I miss…, her cat protested.

We will die anyway. They have found us—and the Heart, Mia whispered in resignation.

Her cat turned and hissed when nearly a dozen men entered the sacred chamber from the secret passage. She snarled and flashed her teeth as the last man entered, the High Lord who led them all. His tall form was covered in a cloak, and his face was hidden by the hood. Airabus and two other traitorous palace guards stood by his side.

"Bring her to me and retrieve the Heart," the High Lord ordered.

Mia could feel the determination of her cat as she turned her head and crouched. She realized that her cat was planning on jumping from the stone they were on to the center platform. Such a jump would be extremely difficult from this distance for even the most agile cat. To do it while heavily pregnant and in labor was suicide. Even though she knew they were likely to die anyway, the thought of dying by falling into the acid pool sent terror through her.

No! Mia gasped in horror as her cat leaped.

A strangled cry escaped her when they landed safely and rolled. Her stomach tightened, and she felt warm liquid against her back legs as her water broke. Shifting back into her human form, she placed one hand on her stomach and gripped the edge of the basin with the other.

She pulled herself up and leaned back against it. The traitors hadn't yet reached the first stone of the pool. Turning her gaze to the cloaked figure, she wearily lifted her chin in defiance.

"You will never have the Heart of the Cat," she informed him.

The High Lord reached up with both hands, pulled back his hood, and removed the cover over his mouth that had been distorting his voice. Mia's chin trembled, and her knees threatened to give out, a soft cry of distress escaping her when she saw his face. Raul. How could he be the one who was responsible for the destruction of the Kingdom of the Forest and the death of so many of their people? Her grip on the lip of the basin tightened as she shook her head.

"How could it be you? You... You were... I saw you fall," her throat tightened as overwhelming grief and pain ricocheted through her.

"The Heart of the Cat belongs to us, Mia. Only you can retrieve it. Bring it to me, my love. With this power, we will control the three worlds," he cooed.

"That is not what was agreed upon, Sarafin. The gem is part of the collection," the Curizan warrior standing several feet away growled.

"Kill them," Raul ordered with a wave of his hand, not taking his eyes off of Mia.

"Raffvin warned that you might betray us, Sarafin," the Valdier warrior snarled.

Mia watched as the Valdier warrior shifted. A charcoal and white dragon appeared, blowing flames as the Curizan sent out shafts of shimmering white energy toward the group of Sarafin warriors. They were vastly outnumbered, but their abilities gave them an advantage that Mia had been unaware they possessed.

Several Sarafin warriors retreated from the dragon's flames while two more fought to keep from being impaled by the mysterious spears of white energy. One of the men stepped too close to the edge of the pool. He teetered there before one of the energy spears struck him, knocking him backwards. His screams of pain did not last long as his body dissolved in the shallow pool filled with clear acid.

Mia clumsily crouched and moved around to the far side of the pedestal. Her fingers trembled as she dipped her hand into the clear liquid. Tears blinded her as she lifted the crystal-clear gem out of the basin. She ignored the roar of the dragon and the snarls of the huge cats as they fought back. She looked up at the man who had once held her own heart in his hands.

"Give me the Heart, Mia," Raul quietly ordered, his words barely piercing the pain wracking her body.

"You betrayed me. You betrayed your daughter. You have betrayed your people," she responded, her heart feeling as if it were being ripped from her body.

"We will rule together, my love," Raul murmured, jumping onto the first stone.

Mia looked into his eyes and saw the lie. As much as it hurt to accept, she would not deny what was right in front of her. She and Raul were not on the same side. Her body trembled as she cupped the Heart of the Cat in her hands. She slowly rose to her feet and lifted the stone above her head.

"Aikaterina, I beg of you, save my people," she whispered.

"No!" Raul growled, jumping to another stone.

A white bolt of energy struck her, and Mia bowed in sudden shock, pressing her hand to her chest. Behind Raul, the Curizan returned her shocked gaze with one of triumph. His glee at striking her was short-lived when two Sarafin warriors struck him from behind and sent him into the shallow pool.

The man screamed as the acid wrapped around him and he grabbed at the stone that Raul was standing on. The rock shifted, and Raul slipped. His right arm sank into the liquid up to his elbow as he tried to keep from being catapulted into the pool of acid. Mia swayed as her mate screamed in pain and struggled to keep from falling. He yanked what remained of his arm out of the pool of acid and gripped the stump with his left hand. Swaying, he jumped and clumsily landed on the next step as the Curizan disappeared beneath the clear liquid.

"Mia," he hoarsely choked. Despite the agony he must have been feeling, his glittering eyes were focused not on her face, but on the stone she held above her head. "Together, my love. We will rule the galaxy."

"Never, Raul," Mia whispered. The crystal-clear gem of the Heart of the Cat turned red with her blood as she gripped it with both hands again. "I give this burden to our daughter. I will not live long enough to shoulder it, and there is no other who can. May she live and one day bring peace to our people—a peace that her father sought to destroy."

Mia could feel her life fading away, even as the pain in her abdomen intensified. Tears streamed down her face as her knees buckled, and she sank down to kneel on the platform.

Her eyes remained locked on her mate as he jumped a step closer. The ghastly remains of his partially dissolved arm hung limply by his side, the stump already sealed by the burning acid. She felt like she was seeing him for the first time. He was no longer the handsome warrior who she had admired from afar as she was growing up and then joined with less than a year ago. Instead, she saw him for what he was —a cold, heartless traitor who would sacrifice his own people for power.

"Please… do not let him… harm our… child," she whispered, fighting to live long enough to give her daughter a chance.

Warmth from the Heart of the Cat's magic surrounded her and her soon-to-be-born child as the Goddess answered her plea for help. Waves of gold surrounded the pedestal, protecting them in its warm cocoon. Relief washed through Mia. The Heart of the Cat would be protected. The certainty of that knowledge soothed the tears from her cheeks as she closed her eyes. Her mate could not reach her now.

Please, protect my people… and my cub, Mia silently pleaded as another contraction tightened her body.

They will be safe, a soothing voice said inside her mind.

Mia wasn't sure if the Goddess was really there or if it was the power of the Heart of the Cat. She didn't care which one it might be as long as it protected her people and her child from the man who would have destroyed them all. Her lips parted with a cry as another intense wave of pain surged through her.

She pressed her back to the pillar and panted as pain twisted her lower abdomen. Another strangled cry escaped her, and she reached down between her legs, barely catching the tiny infant that slipped from her body.

Mia opened her eyes and looked at Raul's enraged face. A tired smile parted her lips when she heard her daughter's first cry. She struggled to lift the newborn infant into her arms. Once she did, she cradled the baby against her breast. She immediately felt the love from the spark she had carried in her womb wash over her, giving her renewed strength.

"Trescina, my beautiful, beautiful, little cub," she murmured, caressing the infant's cheek with her fingers.

"Mia…," Raul hoarsely called.

Mia lifted her cold eyes and stared at her mate. "You will never have the Heart of the Cat… or know the love of our daughter," she weakly vowed.

Mia felt the power of the gem she still held in her hand engulf her and Trescina. The golden glow turned to a blood red. Mia fought against the darkness that rose up to swallow them. A strange and wonderful magic enveloped her and Trescina, and she knew the Goddess had answered her plea.

Her life here was over. Her last wish was that her daughter would never experience the heartache of knowing the truth about her father's betrayal, but she feared that was one wish that would be impossible for her to keep—unless Aikaterina sent them far, far away where they would never be found.

CHAPTER ONE

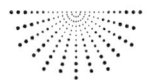

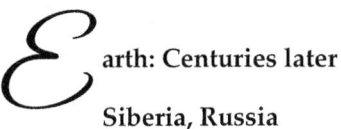arth: Centuries later
Siberia, Russia

Trescina Bukov laughed as she chased her younger half-sister through the forest. Ahead of her, Katarina darted around a thick tree and hid. Trescina slowed and looked around, her eyes twinkling with mischief.

Katarina's breathing sounded loud to Trescina. On silent feet, she crept forward until she rounded the large tree trunk and pounced on her sister, sending her tumbling into the freshly fallen snow. She released a pleased sneeze when Katarina's arms wrapped around her neck, and her sister tightly hugged her.

"Oh, Trescina, I wish I could shift into a tiger like you can," Katarina sighed.

Trescina ran her sandpaper tongue along her sister's cheek. The affectionate caress drew a loud squeal of disgust from Katarina. Trescina gave her sister a toothy grin before she shifted back to her human form and rolled to the side until they were both lying in the snow staring up at the barren trees.

"You were doing good until you bolted. If you had stayed in your hiding spot, I probably wouldn't have found you," Trescina teased.

Katarina sat up and gave her an indignant look. "Of course, you would have found me. You always do, no matter how good a hiding place I find," Katarina good-naturedly complained.

Trescina lifted her legs in the air and then gracefully dropped them so she could roll to her feet. Katarina mimicked her movement. They both brushed the soft snow off of their heavy clothing.

"You are getting much better. It took me twice as long to find you as it did the last time," Trescina said.

"Trescina, why can you shift into a tiger, and I can't?" Katarina asked for the hundredth time. "I can hear you and Momma when you talk, and I can talk to the tigers that Momma and Papa care for, but…." she trailed off sadly.

Trescina wrapped her arms around her sister. Her heart ached for Katarina.

"I don't know. Momma said she would explain when the time was right," Trescina murmured.

They jumped and pulled apart when they heard a series of popping sounds. It almost sounded like firecrackers, but those were not allowed on their property. Trescina stepped in front of Katarina and frowned.

"What was that?" Katarina asked, gripping her arm.

Trescina was about to answer when she heard the sounds again. They both started forward when they heard their mother's cry. Trescina stumbled back a step when Katarina grabbed her arm.

Hide! their mother warned them telepathically.

Momma, Trescina called.

Protect your sister, Trescina, their mother instructed as the popping sounds came again.

Trescina turned and gripped Katarina's gloved hand. Pulling her sister behind her, she ran clumsily through the snow. They made their way deeper into the forest until they reached a river that was partially frozen. Along the bank were the skeletal remains of trees that had become entangled when they washed down during the spring thaw.

"Climb inside and stay there," Trescina said, pushing her six-year-old sister toward the cluster of dead trees.

"What are you going to do?" Katarina asked, climbing between the jagged limbs.

"I have to help Momma. Papa is not here," Trescina replied, picking up several broken branches and covering the spot where Katarina was crouching.

"But... Momma said that we must hide," Katarina protested, grabbing the branch Trescina was about to place in front of her.

Trescina looked at Katarina. They were as different as night and day. Katarina's hair was strawberry red, and her skin was almost as pale as the snow, just like their father. Trescina's long black hair was thick, and its texture reminded her of the mane of the lions she petted at the zoo they had visited a few months before. Her olive complexion was even darker than their mother's.

They had several traits in common, though. They both could communicate with the large cats on the reserve, and they were both stubborn like their mother—at least, that was what their dad liked to say when they got into mischief.

When Trescina heard yelling and a loud, masculine scream rip through the air, she quickly turned and looked back toward their home. Her cat hissed. Fear swelled in her at the thought of her mother facing danger alone.

"I'll be back," Trescina said.

She impatiently looked over her shoulder when she felt Katarina's hand on her arm. She pulled free with a shake of her head and took off at a run through the snow, shifting into her tiger so she could move faster. Ahead of her, she could hear the echoes of popping again.

Dodging trees and ducking under fallen branches, she focused on running as fast as she could. She hoped their father had heard the sounds as well. He had gone to check his hidden cameras along the mountain where he had seen lynx tracks.

Trescina broke through the line of trees onto the tundra. In the distance, she could see flames rising from their house. A flash of black caught her attention. Charging forward, she ran faster than she had ever run before. She emitted a low cry when she saw two men dragging the body of a large Siberian tiger toward a truck.

The flash of black was back. This time her mother attacked one of the men aiming his weapon at a Manul, also called a Pallas cat. This smaller species of cat was a furry wild cat that normally lived in the Altai and Buryatia steppes near the Russian-Mongolian border, but this one had been brought to the reserve after it was injured in a poacher's trap. Trescina and Katarina loved to play with the small cat in the evenings and early mornings after it had been fed.

Momma, behind you, Trescina warned as a second man lifted his rifle to shoot her mother.

Leaping through the air, she rammed her compact body into the man's side. Her claws cut through his leather jacket and into his skin. She twisted, and the powerful attack, combined with her momentum, knocked the man off-balance. With a sharp report, the rifle fired harmlessly into the air instead of at her mother.

The man fell to the ground. Trescina rolled several times before she surged back to her feet. Her cat hissed a warning when one of the men turned from the back of the truck with a gun and aimed it at her.

She darted forward as the man she had knocked down sat up. The man from the truck fired three rounds at her. One hit the ground in front of her while the other two struck the man she had attacked earlier as she moved behind him.

The man jerked each time a bullet hit his chest. A loud curse exploded from the man standing next to the shooter. Trescina's mother turned her head and hissed. Blood dripped from her mother's chin and coated parts of her fur.

Trescina, run!! her mother ordered.

"Idiot! You are shooting our men. Kill the cat!" the man growled in Russian.

Trescina turned to follow her mother's orders when she heard the loud repercussion of gunfire. Her mother jerked backwards. At the same time, the man who had fired the shots earlier convulsed. She looked up and saw her father running across the open area toward them.

"Vlad, let's go," another man said in Russian, coming around the side of the truck.

"Not without that cat. Look at her coat. Her pelt will be worth a fortune on the black market! I want the cub as well. We can sell them both," Vlad ordered.

Both men ducked when her father shouldered his rifle, aimed, and fired at them. The man next to Vlad lifted the rifle in his hand to return fire. Trescina saw her mother leap forward, her front claws extended. Trescina backed up as her mother drove the man back against the truck. Her powerful jaws clamped around the man's neck. The rifle in his hand fell to the ground as he struggled to break free.

No! Trescina cried when she saw Vlad pull a machete out of the back of the truck.

She watched helplessly as Vlad drove the long blade through her mother's ribs. Her mother stiffened and released her grip on the man's throat. Vlad pulled the machete free and stabbed her mother again.

Her mother emitted a loud yowl of pain before she crumpled to the ground. Grief seared through Trescina, and she attacked with everything she had in her small body. Her teeth sank into the man's arm near his elbow. He twisted and punched her in the side near the top of her ribs. She clawed at his chest in a desperate attempt to break free.

He struck her again, this time against the side of her head. The stunning blow caused her to release her grip on his arm. His long fingers gripped the skin of her nape and he held her up and away from him. She braced for another blow when he lifted his hand. The force of his backhand snapped her head to the side, causing black dots to dance in front of her.

Darkness fogged the corner of her vision before she shook it away. Staring at the ground, an uncontrollable sob tore from her throat when she saw the dark blood staining her mother's side.

Fight, Trescina, her mother weakly ordered. *Use your claws.*

Trescina could hear her mother struggling to breathe. She whimpered again when the man pulled her close, using her as a shield against her father's assault.

The man next to Vlad straightened, lifting one hand to grip his ravaged throat. There was a loud report from her father's rifle, and the man's eyes suddenly widened. He looked down at his chest. A circle of blood began to bubble from the bullet hole in his heart.

Trescina cried out when Vlad's hand tightened on her neck as he backed around the side of the truck. Her father dove for cover when Vlad lifted his bleeding arm and fired several shots from his pistol. Trescina's cat hissed in rage. These men—especially this one—had come to destroy her small, happy family for nothing more than greed.

She erupted in a wild frenzy, raking her back claws down the man's chest, opening up new deep cuts near the ones she had already inflicted. The man moved to put more space between them, and Trescina took advantage, striking him across his left cheek, leaving four lines of deep cuts from his cheekbone to his chin.

He opened his hand and dropped her. When she landed on the ground, he shot out his booted foot and struck her in the side, sending her flying back against the heated stone of her burnt home. Trescina lifted her head and watched with dazed eyes as the man named Vlad jumped into the truck that had been left running.

She flinched when rock, snow, and grit from the spinning back tires struck her face and chest. She struggled to her feet and shifted back to human form. She staggered on trembling legs over to her mother where she lay panting. Dropping to her knees, she bent over her mother's limp body as her father slid to a stop and knelt beside her.

"Oh, my beautiful love. You must hold on," her father pleaded softly in Russian as he moved his hand to the deep wound on her side. "Please, my love."

Trescina caressed the soft fur of her mother's face with trembling hands. Her father's words passed over her numb mind as he frantically tried to stem the blood flowing from her mother's side. Tears blurred her vision when her mother's body shimmered, and she shifted into her human form.

"Momma," Trescina choked as she ran her fingers along her mother's cheek.

"Trescina… where's… Katarina?" her mother forced out in a voice filled with pain.

Trescina reached down and grabbed her mother's hand. She pressed the back of her mom's cold fingers against her damp cheek. She released a trembling breath as she fought to answer.

"She's safe. I hid her down near the river," Trescina responded in a soft, tearful voice.

Her mother pulled her hand free and reached for the chain around her neck. When the necklace caught under her mother's shirt, Trescina reached down and helped her pull it out.

"Take it," her mother ordered.

Trescina looked at her mother in confusion for a moment before she clumsily unhooked the clasp and pulled it free. She held the glowing red gem between the palms of her hands. Looking up at her father, she silently begged him for help.

"Ivan...," her mother's voice was barely audible.

Trescina watched her father scoot closer and grip her mother's hand. Tears coursed down his face as he lifted the pale fingers to his lips. His own hands were stained with her blood.

"Protect them.... My people...," her mother whispered.

Ivan nodded. "I will, my love. I will protect them with my life. Your people will always be safe," he vowed.

A tender smile curved her mother's lips before she turned and looked at Trescina again. A flash of pain swept across her face, and she tried to draw in a breath. Trescina could see the light fading from her mother's eyes.

"You must... keep our secret. Our people....," her mother's voice faded to silence as she released her last breath.

"Momma," Trescina cried.

She bent forward and pressed her cold cheek to her mother's. Harsh sobs made it hard to catch her breath. She wrapped her arms around her mother's neck and rocked back and forth, calling for her.

"Momma...," another soft voice called.

Trescina lifted her head and looked at Katarina. She must have felt their mother's passing. Their father turned and held out his arms. Katarina ran forward with a sob.

"I'm so sorry, Mia. I should have been here," their father muttered as he cradled Katarina in his arms. "I will protect our daughters. I swear I will protect them with my life."

Vladimir Mirvo pressed the smooth sleeve of his worn brown leather jacket against his ravaged cheek. A low curse escaped him when he felt the sting of his ripped flesh. The tiger cub's claws were like razor blades. They had laid his flesh open as smoothly as a surgeon's scalpel. The damn cat had inflicted wounds on his face and chest that he would carry for the rest of his life.

He tightened his right hand on the steering wheel of the truck when its back-end started to slide. He fought for control of the bulky vehicle on the slushy, mud-covered road. He eased back on the accelerator to keep from losing control. Vlad shot a quick look at the side mirror to see if he had put enough distance between himself and the man who had unexpectedly appeared. Now several hundred feet from the house, he released an irritated sigh. He was the only man out of a team of five to survive what should have been a simple mission.

He grimaced in pain when he hit a deep rut, jarring his body and reminding him again of the deep cuts to his chest. Mud splashed over the hood and coated the windshield and side windows, nearly blocking his view of the slippery road in front of him. With an impatient flick of his wrist, he turned on the windshield wiper. Globs of mud smeared across the already dirty glass, creating half-moon streaks that allowed him limited visibility.

He reached down and gripped the window crank.

He turned the lever and quickly rolled the window down so that he could see behind him. In the reflection, he saw the blond-haired man who had shot two of his men kneeling next to the large tiger that had attacked them shortly after they had arrived. He started to refocus on the road when it hit him that there was something odd about the scene behind him.

He eased up on the gas pedal, opened the window, and wiped at the side mirror. He ignored the pain that exploded through his cheek when the frigid wind swept across the open wounds. He stared at the image reflected in the mirror. A young, dark-haired girl was bent over the still figure of the large, black cat. When he had first glanced in the mirror as he pulled away, there had been the tiger cub next to the tiger.

He cursed when he glanced up at where he was driving just in time to see the narrow road wind to the left. He jerked the steering wheel in time to make the turn, and could now no longer see what he wanted to in the mirror. Slamming on the brakes, he shifted the truck into park and grabbed the binoculars from the floorboard between the two front seats.

He pulled the door handle and practically fell out of the truck in his haste. Running up the side of the slope, he fell to his stomach and lifted the binoculars to his eyes. He swept over the field of vision until he narrowed in on the house that he had set on fire when they first arrived.

Vlad followed the ground from the edge of the house until he found what he was searching for. The man knelt beside the body of the large cat. Adjusting the focus, he moved to the dark, curly-haired little girl who was bending over the tiger.

Confusion swept over him. Where was the tiger cub? Where had the little girl come from? It had not been long enough for a girl to appear and a tiger to disappear—not by conventional means. There had been something off about this from the beginning. Adjusting the focus on the binoculars again, he returned his attention to the injured black tiger. A sudden wave of shock and disbelief swept through him. Instead of the tiger, a woman lay between the man and child now. He focused on the woman. He could see blood staining her clothing.

"Impossible!" he muttered.

He cursed in frustration at not being able to get a clearer view. A shiver ran through him when he saw the little girl lift something between her hands. He pulled the binoculars away and looked at the snow when he felt a drop of liquid fall from his chin. Bright red blood stained the pristine white, reminding him of the sharp claws that had raked his cheek.

"They are unnatural beasts who must be cursed," he muttered as he scooted backwards and up onto his knees before pushing off the ground.

His mind swirled with the images he had just witnessed as he walked back to the truck. His gaze narrowed on the dead tiger in the back. He lifted the tailgate and secured the canvas to make sure no one could see what he had in the back. The Siberian tiger's pelt would bring him a small fortune on the black market, but he was now thinking of something that could bring him much, much more.

A grim smile curved his lips. A child who could change into a tiger would bring him great wealth. There were buyers all over the world that would pay a fortune to own someone as rare as she was. He would return once he had unloaded his cargo and had his face stitched up. That would give him time to do research on the identity of the blond-haired man and recruit the help he would need to capture the child.

CHAPTER TWO

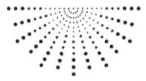

resent day:

Deep in the Shrouded Forest of Sarafin

Walkyr moved through the rebel encampment with confidence. Dressed as a mercenary, he kept all but his eyes covered, which did not reflect their true color thanks to Arrow Ha'darra's new invention. His older brothers had been right when they said the Curizan were masters of technology.

Prince Jazar 'Arrow' Ha'darra had worked closely with Walkyr's younger brother, Pallu, to develop the special contact lenses that allowed him to see in the harshest conditions, no matter which form he took, while also covering the telltale color of his eyes. Now instead of silver eyes that would have revealed his royal lineage, they were dull, gunmetal gray.

Walkyr watched a tall man step out of the shadows between two skimmers. The man didn't slow down as he neared Walkyr; instead, he veered to the left, away from a group of men who were complaining about their living conditions. On silent feet, Walkyr moved away from the men, too, pulling his small disruptor from the belt at his waist. He pressed a button on its side, and the security shield in front of him opened, allowing him to pass through it into the thick forest on the other side.

The day after their small group had arrived, they had erected the shield. It had not been soon enough, however. Several men had been attacked by some of the more savage native beasts. Walkyr had witnessed one of the attacks. He'd never seen such creatures on Sarafin before. These beasts must have evolved in this forest only.

Walkyr briefly looked over his shoulder and shook his head. He knew that he was being followed. Once out of sight of the perimeter of the compound, he shape-shifted into his leopard form and took to the trees. He used the branches to move above the ground. Several yards into the forest, he heard the snap of a branch breaking. He crouched on the thick tree limb and waited.

He swept his gaze over the shadows below him. The tall ferns almost concealed the person, but his contact lenses helped him see the man's outline. He silently snorted and shook his head again —*amateur*. He tensed his muscles for a moment before he jumped down, landing on the creature behind the familiar man who had been following him.

"*Cat's balls,* Walkyr. Don't sneak up on me like that," Pallu hissed, twisting around and lowering the weapon in his hand.

Walkyr released the large lizard that had been about to attack his brother. With a deft swat of his massive paw, he sent the creature flying through the air and into the high ferns. A single bite from the creature would have paralyzed his brother in his two-legged form. Since they preferred fresh meat, the large lizard would have eaten Pallu while he was still alive. With a thought, Walkyr shifted to human form and looked at his brother with a raised eyebrow.

"How you've managed to live this long is beyond me," Walkyr dryly retorted.

Pallu grinned at his brother. "I was always the smartest and luckiest out of all of us. Besides, remember what Riley said? We have nine lives, so I have many more before I am in true danger of dying," he replied.

"She also said the taser wouldn't hurt. How did that go for you?" Walkyr asked with a raised eyebrow.

Pallu grimaced and rubbed his chest at the memory of his new sister's tiny weapon. He had made the mistake of teasing Riley about the tiny toy shortly after the ceremony of marriage between Riley and his oldest brother. He really should have listened to Viper's warning. After all, his big brother wasn't known for a sense of humor or a tendency to over-exaggerate. Riley's little toy had given him a deeper appreciation of the danger in taunting his two new sisters.

"Not good. I'm just thankful that Vox refused to give Pearl her weapon back. Viper said it is ten times more painful," he admitted with a wry grin.

Walkyr chuckled. Pearl St. Claire was the grandmother of Riley and Tina. The fiery woman wore as much leather as a Sarafin warrior and had the heart of one as well.

For a brief moment, a wave of envy swept through Walkyr before he pushed it away with a shudder. Out of six brothers, two had already fallen for human women. Perhaps the term *fallen* was too harsh. Vox and Viper had found their mates, something that Walkyr had never thought would happen—especially for Vox. Vox might have grumpily lived out his whole life mated to the Valdier princess his parents had chosen if Riley hadn't swept him off his feet first—or more accurately, saved his life, then tasered him to the ground. Vox and Viper's mates were quite unusual, most likely because their planet was so distant and isolated.

"Have you discovered any new information?" Walkyr asked, pulling his mind away from mates and his brothers.

Pallu shook his head in frustration. "Nothing. I'm beginning to think coming here was a waste of time. I think we should kill the lot of them and return home," he replied with a disgusted shake of his head. "If this is the best the traitors can recruit, then we shouldn't have anything to fear."

Walkyr looked back toward the encampment. He reached up and rubbed his chest. His cat was pacing within their shared mind. He was surprised that Pallu didn't have the same intense feeling that something important was about to happen. Of course, Pallu didn't have the field experience that he and Viper had. Pallu's passion had always been for technology, research, and weapons. That was one reason Walkyr had been reluctant for Pallu to join him on this mission.

"There is something we are missing. My cat is anxious," Walkyr murmured.

Pallu frowned and looked at him with concern. "What do you think it is?" he quietly asked.

Walkyr turned and looked deep into the forest. There was something there. He needed to go farther into the forest. He could sense its pull on his cat. His gaze narrowed when he noticed a shimmer of golden light—a floating *ball* of light. It felt like it was beckoning to him.

"Notify Vox about the encampment," Walkyr murmured, his eyes still focused on the forest and the orb.

"What are you going to do?" Pallu asked in concern.

Walkyr looked at his brother. "The scroll Viper found said there was a palace in this forest that held the secrets to the Heart of the Cat. I'm going to find it," he quietly replied.

Pallu looked at the dense barrier of swirling fog. Walkyr could feel his brother's concern. Even with the special lenses, finding his way would be nearly impossible. He could easily become disoriented and lost—or worse, become food for one of the creatures that lived within the fog.

"I can relay a message to Vox and join you," Pallu countered.

Walkyr hesitated. He looked at the forest again before he nodded his head. The others at the camp would assume that they had been attacked and eaten or that they had deserted the group. At least they would if any of the others even noticed they were gone. They had drawn little attention from the disgruntled band so far. With a sharp nod of his head, Walkyr reluctantly agreed.

"Notify Vox," he quietly instructed.

Walkyr waited as Pallu contacted their brother. He could hear Vox's quiet inquiries as Pallu told him that Eldora, Vox's former lover, had spoken the truth. Walkyr felt little sympathy for his brother's former lover. She had betrayed her people. She'd said she had done it to protect her family. In the end, someone had poisoned Eldora to silence her, but before she died, she tried to repair a small part of the damage she had done by sharing her knowledge of this hidden camp, and warning them that the threat to their family and people was still very much alive.

"Watch your backs. I've ordered the attack team to take the encampment," Vox stated.

"The men said they were waiting for the High Lord. I overheard several of the men talking. They said he should have been here days ago. They are concerned that he has not arrived," Pallu replied.

"Bragnar must have warned the High Lord that we were closing in on him before he attacked Viper. I want this finished, Pallu. The Heart of the Cat must be found and secured," Vox ordered.

Walkyr snorted and looked over at the screen. "Your wish is easier said than done, brother. Even with the Curizan's technology, we can barely see more than a few feet in front of our faces," he retorted.

Pallu nodded in agreement. "IF we don't get lost… or eaten… and those are two big IFs, we still have to find this forgotten palace and decipher the message that was left behind in the scroll," he added in a dry tone.

"Between the two of you, you'll figure out where it is," Vox responded with confidence. "We are departing now and will meet you at the encampment when you get back. Out."

Walkyr saw Pallu blink at the blank screen before he bared his teeth at it. Walkyr quietly chuckled and shook his head. Where Vox charged into things, Pallu planned everything out and used technology to resolve an issue as much as possible. Each had their special skills. However, those skills came with different attitudes. Vox was bossy and impatient. Viper tended to be short-tempered, but his actions were well thought out. Walkyr's other two brothers, Gable and Qadir, liked to work as a team. Walkyr, on the other hand, preferred to work alone.

"You should stay here," Walkyr quietly said.

Pallu frowned. "I thought we agreed that I should go with you? Don't you think I can keep up?" he responded with a slight growl of frustration.

Walkyr turned and looked at his younger brother. His gaze dropped to the screen in Pallu's hand. Lifting an eyebrow, he grinned.

"I changed my mind," Walkyr said. "This mist is heavier than it looks. One of us needs to stay here if I'm going to find my way back. Vox would be pissed if we both got lost," he reasoned.

The indignant look in Pallu's eyes faded as the rationale behind his request sank in, then Pallu pulled a small black bag from one of the pouches in his utility belt. Pallu opened the bag and pulled a tiny black disk the size of a small seed from it. He balanced it on the tip of his finger before he carefully tapped his finger to the center of the screen. Once the screen changed, Pallu held the small disk out to him. Walkyr gingerly swept the black dot off of his brother's finger and looked at it with a frown.

"What is this?" he asked, looking up at his brother.

"These are your tickets back, so don't lose them," Pallu replied, holding out the bag. "Arrow and I developed them. You need to create a trail of them along the way. The device I gave you is crucial. It is connected to my system. Press it to your neck."

Walkyr gave his brother a skeptical look before he pressed the dot to his neck. He hissed when he felt a slight prick to his skin. Pallu grinned at his reaction.

"You could have warned me that it had a bite," he dryly commented.

Pallu shrugged. "We installed micro-hooks to keep it attached to your skin, even if you shift. The device also has biometric enhancements that allow for individual user identification. I added that function. This way it won't come loose, and you will be less likely to lose it, considering it is so small," he explained.

"So, I take the others and scatter them as I go along? How will I know where they are?" he asked.

"They will emit a vibration. Arrow originally wanted to use heat, but I told him that wouldn't work. The last thing I wanted was to leave any more of a heat signature than you would normally put out. It would make it too easy to track you. Plus, how would you know if it was the locator or your own body? I also didn't want anything that made a noise. It wouldn't be good to have it go off and alert others. Instead, I went for a pulse. The closer you get to one of the markers, the faster it will pulse," Pallu explained.

Walkyr nodded, impressed with his brother's creativity. "How many markers are there?" he asked, opening the bag to peer inside.

"A few thousand, but you need to make sure you place them no more than five hundred steps apart. Any further and they lose their effectiveness. Oh, and you only have two sunrises to return. Something that size has a limited power source. They will deactivate and dissolve after that to prevent anyone from finding them," Pallu cautioned before he glanced down at the screen he was holding. "We are about to have company, and it isn't one of ours. Go—I'll take care of them."

"How do you know someone's coming?" Walkyr demanded, looking in the direction of the encampment.

"I added trackers to the liquor this morning. This way we would know if anyone tried to escape," Pallu chuckled as he slid the small screen into his pocket and pulled out his weapon.

"It is better to observe than attack. We wouldn't want them alerting any of the others before the security forces arrive," Walkyr replied.

Pallu gave him a disappointed nod before he replaced his pistol and looked up. Walkyr shifted and took to the trees. A second later, Pallu did the same. They watched two of the rebels from the encampment approach. It was obvious both men were extremely nervous.

"I can't see my hand in front of my face," the man in front replied.

"Zire, it isn't your hand that you should be looking at. *Something* disrupted the shield. Pay attention so we can tell the commander this section is clear," the second man retorted.

"Clear? No one can see a thing out here. How would we know if it was clear or not? Anyone stupid enough to venture away from the shield deserves what they get. I say we return while we can and tell the commander that we found nothing," Zire growled.

Walkyr watched the two men turn. They had only taken a few steps when nearby explosions rocked the ground. The squadron of Vox's warriors had arrived.

With a powerful leap, Walkyr landed on top of Zire while Pallu took out the other warrior. He sank his teeth into Zire's throat, and the weight of his leopard trapped the struggling male under him. He had made sure to avoid the main artery running along Zire's neck. He wanted the man alive long enough to interrogate him. Out of the corner of his eye, he could see Pallu quickly shifting back to human form and leaning to the side to spit.

"*Cat's balls*! Walkyr, watch out! They have poison," Pallu warned, wiping a hand across his mouth.

Walkyr jerked his fangs out of the man as the acidic taste hit his taste buds. His cat recoiled from the poison. Shifting, he also spat on the ground. He could still feel a slight numbness on his tongue. Spitting again, he used his foot to turn the man over onto his back.

"They didn't even try to resist," Walkyr growled.

"Here, put this on your tongue and let it dissolve," Pallu ordered, holding out a thin blue strip.

"What is it?" Walkyr muttered, taking the strip and placing it on his tongue.

"It is a counter-agent for the poison. It is a new technology. The strip analyzes the poison and releases the correct reagent to neutralize the poison. I'm still working on it, but it has successfully counteracted the most common poisons and the one Eldora died from," Pallu said, looking up as dozens of troop carriers flew overhead. "It looks like Vox sent half the guards."

Walkyr looked at his brother with an expression filled with skepticism. "You're working on it? I can't tell you how much confidence that gives me," he sarcastically pronounced. "How did you know to bring a counter agent?"

Pallu chuckled. "If you had spent an afternoon with Riley and Tina, you would understand. I swear those two had me ready to pack up my entire lab! Have you seen the bag that Riley carries? It is incredible. She has something in it for every situation. Tina was the one who said that they may try to use poison to keep from being caught. Riley said they use that in all the old-time movies. I asked them to make a list of these movies they are always talking about. Trelon Reykill may have some of them," Pallu mused.

Walkyr shook his head. His two new sisters were from a world called Earth. Zoran Reykill, King of the Valdier, had crashed on their planet a few years ago. Valdier was home to the dragon-shifting species that the Sarafin had once fought during the Great War.

The only thing he knew about Earth was that it had somehow managed to survive without imploding, despite Trelon's mate Cara, as well as Riley, Tina, Pearl St. Claire, and Ruby, Tina's chicken. That was miraculous considering the chaos that the women tended to leave behind. Having met all of the above, all he could say was he felt sorry for his older brothers and Prince Trelon.

"It looks like the situation is contained here. I will return. Make sure that my skid is left behind," Walkyr ordered.

"Two sun rotations, Walkyr. Don't forget. I'll wait here for you," Pallu reminded him as another explosion rocked the ground.

Walkyr nodded. "I'll find the Heart of the Cat and return," he promised.

He gripped the small bag in his hand and pulled his blade out. Slicing a tiny hole close to the bottom of the bag, he gripped the top of it between his teeth. In seconds, he shifted into a large black leopard with dark blue spots that formed an intricate pattern throughout his coat.

Walkyr ignored the battle behind him. His brothers could deal with the traitors who thought they could destroy the royal family. His focus was on finding the Heart of the Cat.

Small markers fell through the small hole in the bottom of the bag and scattered along the ground as he ran through the thick mist. The lenses Pallu and Arrow had developed allowed him to see just far enough ahead to swerve around the obstacles in his path. His cat warned him when it sensed danger, and he took to the trees, never breaking his stride as he followed that small golden orb beckoning to him.

CHAPTER THREE

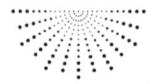

"How long does Walkyr have?" Vox demanded, pacing back and forth inside the rebel command tent.

Pallu glanced down at the screen in his hands. "Eighteen hours. He'll make it," he said.

"He'd better. Keep me posted," Vox ordered.

Pallu nodded and his older brother pulled open the flap to the tent and stepped outside. Pallu inhaled deeply and released it slowly. It was going to be a long eighteen hours.

"What's wrong?" Arrow asked, looking up from the console where he was working.

Pallu walked over and sat down on a crate next to the computer system Arrow was setting up. He glumly stared down at the screen in his hand before he held it out to Arrow. The Curizan frowned and took the tablet.

"There's nothing there. What am I supposed to be looking for?" Arrow asked, looking up at him.

Pallu took the tablet back and waved it at the other man. "Exactly!

There is nothing there, but there should be something there. A whole line of somethings and a moving dot! Walkyr is wearing one of the sensors we created. He left with a bag of markers that should be lighting up the screen. Instead, there is nothing! No markers, no moving sensor, no way to track and find him if he doesn't make it back in time," he growled, tossing the tablet onto the crate beside him.

Arrow shook his head. "That's impossible. We tested it. There must be something wrong with your tablet," he insisted.

Pallu looked at Arrow with a raised eyebrow. "There's not, but you're welcome to try yours. The tracker's identification signal was showing up before I gave it to Walkyr. Even if it malfunctioned, the markers should still register on the map. You try to explain how a thousand of them can all go bad at once," he retorted.

Pallu folded his arms across his chest and watched Arrow run the program through his own tablet—again and again. Arrow's initial disbelief quickly changed to a growl of aggravation, and he glared at Pallu.

Pallu raised his hands. "I'm just as frustrated as you are. We tested the device extensively, and it didn't fail a single trial," he reminded Arrow.

"We need to test it again. There has to be some reason for why it's not showing up," Arrow grumbled.

Pallu thought for a moment. He looked up at the doorway and the dense mist beyond, swirling around outside of the encampment.

The shields had been restored once the camp was overtaken. Unfortunately, the few men who hadn't fought to the death took poison just like the two he and Walkyr had encountered earlier. Fortunately for Vox, Pallu had been prepared and managed to give one of the traitors an antidote before the poison had a chance to kill the man. Of course, the man was still in critical condition and had to be transported back to the city for additional healing before he could be interrogated.

"Do you think the mist is causing the interference?" Pallu mused.

Arrow thought for a moment before he shrugged. "It is possible. After all, none of the scanners have been able to penetrate it. We were working on the assumption that the markers would eliminate all interference by placing a line-of-sight tracking system. Since there were no disruption devices or magnetic fields detected, we assumed that the markers placed at regular intervals would overcome the issue," Arrow responded.

"We should test the theory. If it is an issue, we have less than eighteen hours to figure out how to correct it, otherwise, Walkyr could be in serious trouble," Pallu stated, grabbing the tablet next to him and rising to his feet.

Arrow nodded and looked out across the thick mist. "If he isn't already," Arrow muttered.

∽

Walkyr jumped over a fallen tree, keeping a steady pace as he followed the glowing orb. His mind drifted as he ran. He replayed the information he knew over and over in his mind in an effort to connect any pieces of the puzzle that he might have missed.

He broke down the data into three separate categories to make it easier to distinguish the facts from the myths. First, he focused on his own personal experience. He sorted through everything he knew about the Great War, including who and what had been behind the start of the conflict.

Centuries ago, a secret group of men and women led by Valdier, Curizan, and Sarafin nobles and their followers united to form a secular faction. The group had used their positions to undermine the royal families that ruled over the three worlds.

The group called themselves *The Enlightenment*. Their members were made up of rebels from a variety of different species. What concerned Walkyr was that they had recruited members of each royal family as well. Later, it was discovered that trusted warriors of the family had infiltrated and betrayed the people they were sworn to protect.

The group had used the members' positions to begin a battle that had led to the Great War—a conflict between the three worlds that had lasted for centuries. It was not until a chance battle between Creon Reykill of the Valdier, Ha'ven Ha'darra of the Curizan, and Walkyr's older brother, Vox, that the treachery had been uncovered. By then, thousands of warriors from each world had perished.

Personally, Walkyr questioned the current belief that the Valdier royal, Lord Raffvin, had been the leader of the entire operation. He had also been skeptical about the notion that only a few members of *The Enlightenment* still existed. The information he had discovered since his arrival confirmed his suspicion that the men from the encampment were in just one of several such groups searching for historical and/or mythical items of great importance and power.

He agreed that the deaths of Raffvin, a Valdier Royal, and Ben'qumain, a member of the Curizan royal family, had been a blow to the faction's regime. However, the recent attack on his brother, Viper, proved that the group had not abandoned their ambitions.

Walkyr also didn't believe that the only *Sarafin* members of the group were Vox's two ex-lovers. Each of the females had died—Pursia by suicide and Eldora by poison—before she could tell them much. The other traitor, Bragnar, had been a low-level warrior who had died during the attack on Viper.

The men back at the rebel camp had been waiting for someone of importance. They suspected the person was the mysterious High Lord —the man whose face they had yet to see—but what if they were mistaken? What concerned him the most was that even without the information from the scroll, whoever had ordered the men to set up camp appeared to be one step ahead of the Sarafin Royal brothers. That meant there had to be a leak somewhere—and the only person that came to mind was the Curizan named Arrow. As much as he hated the idea, he couldn't help asking himself if it was possible that Ha'ven's half-brother was a spy for *The Enlightenment.*

I think a detailed look into Arrow's background and any close associates might be necessary, he ruminated.

He decided to push the idea of Arrow's possible involvement to the back of his mind for the moment. Instead, he turned his focus on what he remembered of the legends that he had learned about as a child.

The legends talked about where the Sarafin had come from and how they were given the ability to shape-shift. The legend claimed that what had been freely given to his people could also be taken away.

It was difficult to believe in such a thing with all of the technology at their disposal, but the possibility that it was true was difficult to ignore. He had seen many strange things in his life, and it was certainly possible that the 'Goddess' belonged to a rare species who had far more advanced technology than their own.

He jumped up on a log and sprang onto a low branch. Working his way up higher into the canopy, he hopped from one branch to another as his mind processed the last bit of information that he knew existed. The discovery of a scroll hidden deep in the archives had pieced together gaps between the facts and the myths.

It was said that a survivor of the Great War wrote it. This scroll documented the events of the attack. It told of a Princess, heavily pregnant with her first child, who was brutally betrayed by the one she loved. In desperation, Princess Mia had sacrificed her life and the life of her newborn child to keep her people safe. According to the scroll, Princess Mia used the powers of the Heart of the Cat and then vanished. The problem was—no one knew what happened to the Princess and the Heart of the Cat. The scroll only said that Princess Mia was helped—by a Goddess.

And now I am following a golden orb through a thick mist to a mythical kingdom that hasn't been seen in centuries, he thought with a silent snort.

Better than running in circles and lost, his cat chuckled in response as it closed the distance between Walkyr and the orb.

CHAPTER FOUR

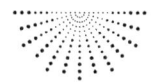

Several hours later, the hair along Walkyr's back bristled and his cat hissed as it sensed an unknown threat coming up from behind and below him. He perched on the thick branch of a tree he had climbed a few moments ago and held perfectly still. The tree shook. Whatever was coming, it was large.

His eyes narrowed when he finally saw what his cat had sensed—pactors! How in the hell those beasts were on Sarafin he had no idea. They were mean, disagreeable creatures who ate just about anything—including people. The Antrox, a slender insectoid species known for their mercenary greed, were the only ones he knew that used them for their asteroid mining operations. Keeping them well fed and harnessed was a top priority in those operations, for the safety of everyone—but he did personally know two crazy people who cared about the beasts: Lady Ariel Reykill and the Twin Dragons' mate, Melina.

He closely observed the leader of the herd. There was something—or he should say someone—else down there. Partially hidden by the trunk of the lead pactor, Walkyr could see the end of a walking stick.

Walkyr crouched, turned, and followed the creatures. He silently jumped from branch to branch until the tree line ended near a wide river. The group of pactors stepped onto the rocky embankment and down into the river. Only when every beast had waded into the river did Walkyr turn his attention to the lone figure carrying the walking stick.

Disappointment washed through him when he saw it was a young, hesitant pactor with a slender branch held in his trunk. Walkyr watched as the largest pactor turned and released a series of soft grunts. The young pactor reluctantly walked toward the river and tentatively entered the water. Walkyr's cat snickered when the juvenile pactor batted the stick at the pactor in charge before turning its back to it.

I'm glad you think they're amusing. You do realize that they wouldn't think twice about eating us, don't you? Walkyr dryly mentioned.

His cat snorted, as if it were insulted. Walkyr was about to stress his point—but a movement out of the corner of his eye caught his attention. The golden orb floated several yards away from where he was crouched. Walkyr released an exasperated groan when he felt his cat's response.

The damn thing thought this was a game! Rising to his feet, he shook his head a little to dislodge a few markers before running along the branch. He tensed and leaped through the air, landing on a branch in the next tree. His back legs slipped a bit on the branch and he flicked his tail back and forth to adjust his balance. He dug his claws into the stiff bark.

Ahead of him, the orb continued to float just out of his reach. He had been following the thing for hours now. He jumped from one limb to another until he came to an area farther up river where he would have to leave the safety of the high ground so that he could cross to the opposite river bank.

At least no pactor here, his cat reasoned.

Thank the Goddess for small favors, Walkyr growled.

He scanned the river bank before he hopped from branch to lower branch until he was close enough to safely jump the rest of the way to the ground. His massive paws sank into the moist, leaf-covered soil.

The orb paused as Walkyr hesitated to move out into the open. After making sure there was no immediate threat, Walkyr padded across the uneven rocky ground to the edge of the river, and waded in. It wasn't long until the chilly water was deep enough that Walkyr needed to swim. With his back legs he pushed off the last bit of river bed he could reach and began paddling across the wide river.

The current was swift, pulling and pushing him downstream. He pumped his powerful front and back legs like pistons, cutting a path through the current. He kept his gaze on the floating orb that hovered above the far bank.

Out of the corner of his eye, he could see a group of boulders rising out of the water. His cat hissed, knowing that he was in danger of colliding with them. Walkyr swam faster.

A curse exploded through his mind when he realized that he wouldn't make it to an area shallow enough to brace his feet. A hole in the riverbed caused the water to swirl fiercely, and Walkyr was caught in the whirlpool. The strong current spun his cat in a dizzying whirl of wet fur and extended claws. He went under, and the churning of the water pushed his cat down to the riverbed.

His cat pushed off the rocky bottom and struggled toward the surface. Walkyr hissed out a warning when he saw that they were going to collide with the group of boulders. His cat twisted so that he was facing the danger and managed to impact with all four paws against the rocks. Unfortunately, one of his back feet slipped on the algae-covered rocky surface and became caught between two boulders. Pain shot through his leg when the current tried to pull him around.

His cat struggled to lift his head above the water and barely broke the surface. Opening his mouth, he dropped the small bag of markers he was carrying. The cat made a desperate grab for it with his nearest front paw, but it was too late. The small black sack bobbed along the surface before disappearing from sight.

Stuck, his cat snarled, struggling to break free.

His front paws slid off the rocks and his head dipped under the water again. Walkyr scrambled for a hold, but the algae made it impossible to get a good grip while in this form. In desperation, he ordered his cat to shift back into his two-legged form.

With dexterous hands, Walkyr braced against the two rocks that formed the crevice where his foot was caught. It was a much more painful fit than when he was a cat. Holding on, he tilted his head back to draw in a deep breath of air before he sank back down beneath the surface.

He placed his other booted foot against the rock and pushed. The sole of his boot slipped on the rock again and again, which caused his caught foot to become more solidly wedged. His lungs burned with the need for oxygen. Frustration poured through him as he fruitlessly struggled to pull his foot free. He clawed at the rocks, trying to pull them apart, but between the angle and the constant tugging of the current, he couldn't get a good grip.

He began to convulse, his lungs demanding oxygen. His arms trembled as he fought to tilt his head back far enough to break the surface again, but unfortunately, he had slipped lower during his struggles.

Dark spots began to dance before his eyes and then he suddenly felt something soft wrap around his waist. The extra support against his back held him steady against the strong current. The boulders parted, and he yanked his leg free.

Walkyr's head cleared the surface and he took deep, gasping breaths of air. Then he was suddenly lifted clear of the water. He lowered his hands and touched the soft hide-covered flesh wrapped around his waist. Turning his head, his choked gasps froze in his chest, when he saw who—or should he say what—had come to his rescue.

He dangled like a child's doll from the trunk of a large pactor as it carried him to the shore. He glanced over at the other pactors who were rolling the boulders as if they were marbles instead of massive rocks. A squeal drew his attention to the shore, and his mouth dropped open when he saw the baby pactor coming toward him with its trunk up, gaily waving the walking stick like an excited drum major.

It think you is dinner, his cat hissed. It scratched at him to break free.

With a sense of growing apprehension, Walkyr watched the juvenile's mouth open to show large flat teeth made for grinding. Up close he could see the jagged points on the inside that were made for cutting and shredding.

He gripped the gray trunk around his waist and fought to loosen the creature's hold on him. He opened his mouth to snarl in warning but immediately clamped his mouth shut when he was licked from chin to forehead.

Walkyr closed his eyes when he felt a glob of sticky slobber coat his face. He snapped his head back when the juvenile tried to give him the slender branch held in its trunk. Lifting a hand, Walkyr cleared the slime from his eyes before he reached out and grabbed the end of the stick.

He blinked in confusion when the pactor scrambled back several steps and looked at him with an expectant expression. Unsure of what the beast wanted, he tossed the stick away. The juvenile immediately went after the branch, picked it up, and brought it back to him.

"I think I've seen everything now," he muttered in disbelief when the juvenile backed up once again.

It want to play, his cat chuckled.

"Obviously," Walkyr responded with a shake of his head.

He took the branch and tossed it again. The pactor holding him must have been happy with what he was doing because instead of tearing him apart and eating him, the beast set him down on the sandy, rock-covered bank. He took several steps back and faced the group of pactors that had come to his rescue.

He studied the outcropping of boulders where he had nearly died. The two boulders that had trapped his foot were now several feet apart.

There was no denying that the creatures were strong. So, why hadn't they ripped him apart?

He turned his gaze back to the juvenile pactor. His eyes widened when he saw that it had a new distraction—the golden orb. The smaller pactor was squeaking and reaching out its short trunk to the orb that danced slightly out of reach.

The orb floated in a semi-circle, pausing briefly by each pactor before it floated purposefully toward the trees. The pactors parted. Walkyr slowly walked by each of them.

He stopped when the juvenile pactor picked up the branch and held it out to him again. He automatically reached out and accepted the gift. With bemusement, he watched the small herd mosey away along the bank of the river.

Shaking his head, he watched them disappear around the bend before he turned to look back at the orb where it hovered just inside the tree line. He lifted his arm and wiped his face with a wet shirtsleeve. He tightly gripped the branch in his hand and strode forward. The orb moved deeper and deeper into the forest.

The mist changed the farther he traveled away from the rebel camp. When he had first set out, he could barely see his hand in front of his face. Even with the contact lenses, he'd had to move with caution. The mist thinned out even more the deeper he went into the forest. Now, the veil rose to the top of the trees as if it were creating a protective shield over the forest.

Walkyr followed the orb for several more hours. His cat hissed out to him several times that it sensed danger. In his peripheral vision, he caught glimpses of something moving, but whatever was there always remained hidden.

As he covered more ground, Walkyr became concerned about being able to find his way back. Without the markers, he had nothing to guide him but his innate sense of direction. In the mist, that was almost impossible to trust—but there was also… something different about the forest. It felt—alive.

Several times he had turned to study the path he had traversed, only to find thick trees covering the path he was sure he had just followed. His unease grew the farther he went. At one point, he had tried to mark the path by slicing deep gouges into a tree. No sooner had he sliced through the bark than a loud moan filled the air and the ground trembled beneath his feet.

Cursed, his cat hissed.

Walkyr agreed. He could feel the hair on the back of his neck rise, and a shiver ran through him. This was not normal. Trees were alive, but they did not move or feel emotions.

Stay alert, Walkyr ordered.

An hour later, he looked down at the last remains of the broken branch in his hands. He dropped the piece to the ground. He had picked up anything he could find, sometimes even drawing an arrow in the soil to mark the path.

He was about to pick up another branch when he looked up. The roots of the trees nearby were elevated and twined together into an archway. Walkyr brushed his hands together and walked forward. The opening glowed with the orb's golden light, and he could see that the tunnel passed completely through the trunk of a massive tree that rose well over a hundred feet into the air.

Walkyr cautiously moved forward. He reached out and touched the knotted vines that ran along the opening. He was shocked when warmth pulsed from the vines in the otherwise cool interior. Looking down at the ground, he noticed that the path had changed from moist dirt to smooth rock. The sound of his boots on the stone paving echoed in the dark corridor.

Wonder filled him when he saw the intricate carvings along the interior walls. He stepped closer and paused. Lifting his hand, he was about to trace his fingers along the raised designs when his cat hissed a warning.

Not alone.

I saw it, he replied.

There had been a flash of movement out of the corner of his eye. The movement swept past the far opening at the end of the corridor. Turning, he began to stride to the exit but paused to scan the area ahead. He didn't sense any danger, so he continued forward.

Walkyr cautiously stepped out of the tunnel and stared in awe at the scene before him. A large village lay nestled among the thick trees. He swept an astonished gaze from the base of the tree upward to the towering canopy above. The incredible architecture of each home was breathtaking. Some hung from the thick tree branches like huge hives, linked together by bridges made of woven vines. Behind colorful window curtains, he could see the soft glow of lights shining from the huts.

Looking down again, Walkyr studied the structures in front of him. Storefronts had been built in a semi-circle contouring the base of the trees. He frowned when he saw a curtain move in the window of the nearest shop. He took a step toward the building when he heard the soft sound of movement behind.

He swiftly turned and instinctively moved his hand to the blade at his waist. He observed the shadows for a moment. There was no doubt in his mind that he wasn't alone, but, for some reason, whoever lived here did not want to be seen.

The golden orb that was still hovering nearby brightened, drawing his attention. He began walking again. In the trees above and below, shadows followed him. The path ahead of him opened, and he could see lush ferns shimmering in the moonlight.

Walkyr paused at the edge and stared at the largest tree he had ever seen in his life. The scroll that Viper had found described a magnificent tree and stone palace, but Walkyr had never imagined that he would find anything like this. This structure—in fact the entire village—was unlike any other on the planet. There was no doubt in his mind that he had found the home of the Forest Kingdom. The description in the scroll had not done justice to what he had found.

A soft snarl pulled his attention away from the central palace. He narrowed his eyes when he saw several large cats emerge from the darkness. He could hear others behind him.

There are too many to fight, his cat warned.

Then I suggest we don't, Walkyr warily replied.

He turned in a tight circle, gazing at the large array of cats that emerged from the shadows, then he glanced up. For as far as he could see, there were cats' eyes staring at him. Each set was intensely suspicious, eerily reflecting the light.

"I am Prince Walkyr d'Rojah of the Royal House of Sarafin," he announced in a loud, commanding voice as he turned and looked at the two large gray leopards that were taking the lead.

The leopards paused in their tracks. The cat on the right lifted his head, shimmered, and changed into a man. Walkyr found himself staring into the eyes of an old, scarred warrior. He raised an eyebrow when the warrior didn't say anything.

A movement by the scarred warrior's shoulder caught his attention, and Walkyr watched as the orb hovered between them. He narrowed his eyes when it began to expand, and a golden mist spread outward from it, slowly becoming a person. The warrior sank to one knee and bowed his head. Walkyr watched as all the cats did the same. A moment later he understood why.

In front of him, a beautiful Goddess stood serenely watching him. Her body was slender, and she looked like the golden symbiots that the Valdier had by their sides. With a wave of her hand, her appearance changed to that of a Sarafin maiden—only her eyes remained an intense gold color.

He unconsciously took a step forward, drawn by the swirling colors in the golden depths. Mesmerized, he stopped a mere foot in front of her. He swore he could see a reflection of the universe in the depths of her eyes.

"Walk with me, Walkyr," the Goddess quietly commanded.

Walkyr glanced at the cats as they rose to their feet. The old warrior stepped to the side. The Goddess bowed her head to the warrior as she glided past him.

"You are…," Walkyr started to say before he swallowed.

The woman smiled at him. "Yes. I am Aikaterina," she replied.

Walkyr walked beside her, taking in every detail of his surroundings and his companion as they entered the interior of the magnificent tree. In the center was a stone staircase that wound upward. Narrow bridges forked off from the staircase at intervals leading to other sections of the tree. Rivers of green veins that he suspected were the lifeblood of the tree lined the interior. He frowned when he saw the evidence of black scars as if there had once been a massive fire.

"What is going on?" he finally demanded in a harsher tone than he had intended.

Aikaterina paused as she stepped onto the staircase. She slid her hand across the polished banister, caressing the wood. He followed the movement with his eyes.

Thick vine spindles spiraled downward to the natural stone and wrapped around the steps, holding them suspended in the air. Both the woman and the staircase gave the appearance that they were floating and added to the illusion that he was caught in a magical realm instead of a missing kingdom on his world. He shook his head and refocused his gaze on her face.

"You have come searching for the Heart of the Cat, have you not?" she asked.

Walkyr's mouth tightened before he nodded his head. If he hadn't seen the Goddess' transformation and the reverence of the Forest people with his own eyes, he would have refused to respond, but she had led him this far.

"Yes," he answered.

"To find it, you must understand that what you seek is not what you think it is," Aikaterina stated.

Walkyr frowned when she turned away from him and began climbing the staircase. He followed her.

A ghostly warrior ran down the stairs and he startled when the figure ran through him. Turning on the step, he crouched with his hand on the blade at his side.

"What is going on?" he muttered.

He followed the warrior with his gaze. Soon, the area below him was filled with a ghostly battle. His cat clawed at him when a group of spectral Curizan and Valdier surged forward. What infuriated him was the sight of Sarafin warriors attacking their own people. The fighting brought back memories of a battle long ago.

"What you are seeing are memories of what happened here," she replied in a tone laced with sadness.

"Why are you showing me this?" Walkyr demanded with a wave of his hand.

"The past has caught up with the present. It will be up to you to prevent what happens now," Aikaterina said in a calm quiet voice.

A ghostly young woman ran past Walkyr. Tears streaked her grief-stricken face, and she looked fearfully over her shoulder. She was dressed in a long gown. Her dark, curly hair swirled like storm-tossed waves when she turned her head from side to side, searching for a place to hide. Her hand moved down to her rounded stomach.

Walkyr watched as she slipped into an alcove. A moment later, several warriors ran down the corridor. His cat hissed when the men passed through him. He turned when he saw the men come to a stop by a set of large, double doors.

"What happened to her?" Walkyr asked in frustration, wishing he could hear what the men were saying.

"Take my hand, and I will show you," Aikaterina requested.

Her hand no longer looked like it belonged to a Sarafin maiden. She was a Goddess undisguised, and her skin hummed with power beyond anything he had encountered before.

He'd heard tales of the Goddess appearing before others, including close family members. It had been difficult for him to wrap his head around all of the legends and the detailed descriptions in the scroll. In fact, he had been skeptical that the legend of the Heart of the Cat was real—until now.

He turned his thoughts back to the tales told about his people. The stories that were passed down claimed that shortly after the Goddess gave the Heart of the Cat to them, the four brothers had hidden the Heart away to protect it. Many centuries later, the Goddess supposedly revealed the location of the Heart of the Cat to the Queen of the Forest Kingdom's young daughter. The Princess had kept the secret of the gem, but she was betrayed.

Walkyr lifted his hand and placed his palm against Aikaterina's. A wave of disorientation swept through him. He felt like he had transported down from a warship. Shaking his head, he blinked several times to clear his vision. Deep inside, his cat groaned in displeasure.

His eyes widened when he saw that they were in some kind of underground chamber. In the center was a pedestal. Concern washed through him when he saw that the princess was injured. Blood covered her hands and streaked her gown. It took him a moment to realize that she was holding a newly born infant against her bosom.

Nearby, the image shifted. He saw the outline of a man with part of his arm missing staring intently at the woman. His gaze jerked back to the woman and he saw her lips moving, but he couldn't decipher what she was saying. She lifted a red stone above her head. Seconds later, the same shimmering golden light that had guided him through the forest covered the woman and infant. When the light disappeared, the woman and baby were gone.

"You helped her," he stated, staring at the pedestal.

"Yes, but...," Aikaterina said, her voice fading.

Walkyr turned to the Goddess. He frowned when he saw an expression of sadness on her face. The woman had been wounded. Did she and the infant perish? If so, what became of the Heart of the Cat?

"But?" he pressed.

Aikaterina looked at him. Once again, he felt like he was falling into the depths of her eyes. He frowned and took a step closer. He saw… a world. His lips parted when he saw a blue and white planet with a single moon and sun.

"The Heart is in danger. Those that search for the Heart have found where I sent her. You must bring the Heart of the Cat back to your people before it is too late," Aikaterina explained.

"How will I know…?" Walkyr asked, his voice slurring as his mind grew hazy. "What is… happening to me?"

"Find her and bring her home, warrior. They know where she is now. Follow the hunters, and you will find her, but you must get to her first. She has been gone far too long and she needs you," Aikaterina softly murmured.

Walkyr felt the gentle brush of fingers against his furrowed brow. *Her? She? The Heart of the Cat isn't a… her. The Heart of the Cat is a gem. The legend and the scroll….*

The Heart of the Cat is so much more, Aikaterina's soothing voice whispered through his mind.

Walkyr closed his eyes as the words washed through him. For a brief moment, he saw a glimpse of a woman's face before it disappeared. His cat jerked and roared, trying to pull the image back, but it was gone. He swayed, and his mind became foggy. No matter how hard he tried to open his eyes and clear the fog in his brain, he could not. He started to fall, but everything went dark before he hit the ground.

"Walkyr, wake up," Pallu's deep voice pulled at his consciousness.

Walkyr's eyes popped open and he stared at his brother. Pallu was kneeling on one knee in front of him. With a confused frown, Walkyr turned his head and gazed around before focusing on his brother again.

"Where am I?" he asked in a gruff tone.

Pallu rose to his feet and extended his hand. Walkyr grabbed it, and together they brought him to his feet. His mind was beginning to clear, but his confusion remained. Where was he and how the hell had he gotten here?

"You are near the perimeter of the rebel camp," Pallu answered in a voice laced with confusion.

His brother's bewildered tone told him that he would have no answers to any of Walkyr's questions. Walkyr tensed when he noticed a shadowy movement behind his brother. He relaxed when he recognized the Curizan warrior nicknamed Arrow. He rubbed his temple and looked around again. The thick fog made it impossible to see more than a couple of feet in front of him.

"How did I get here?" he suddenly asked.

Pallu's eyes widened in surprise, and he frowned. "You don't remember how you got here?" he probed in a cautious tone.

Arrow stepped forward and ran a scanner over him. He turned to look at the Curizan as Arrow paused near his neck. Walkyr touched the spot on his throat where he felt a slight vibration.

"The tracker is still attached and working like it should," Arrow muttered in a perplexed voice.

Pallu placed his hand on Walkyr's shoulder. "What do you remember? Did you find the Heart of the Cat?" he asked.

The fog suddenly cleared from his mind, and he remembered everything. Walkyr opened his mouth to respond when he heard Vox call out. The three of them turned toward the tent opening when his oldest brother appeared. Walkyr immediately knew something was wrong from the grim expression on Vox's face.

"What is it?" Walkyr demanded.

Vox looked at him. "I hope you found the Heart. If not, we have problems," he stated.

"What's going on?" Pallu wanted to know.

Vox looked at Pallu. "The transport carrying the prisoner you saved from poisoning disappeared on the way back to the city," he explained.

Arrow whistled. "That is pretty ballsy," he replied.

"Ballsy?" Vox muttered with a frown. "Have you been chatting with my mate again?"

Arrow grinned. "I will never confess, but I will say that I like some of the Earth terminology. It is very colorful. Not that I'm admitting anything, but Riley, Tina, and Pearl are much more talkative than Ha'ven's mate, Emma. She can become more vocal if you tease her, though," he replied with a pleased grin before it faded, and he became serious again. "Do you have any information on what happened to the transport?"

Vox nodded. "Viper debriefed the medical technician who escaped. He said that the pilot and co-pilot attacked him and briefly disabled him. He was able to activate the transport's tracking device when he regained consciousness. He then fought with the co-pilot and managed to jump from the transport as it passed over a lake. He's lucky he didn't break his neck. It took him several hours to reach a village where he was able to contact us. The transport had vanished by then, but thanks to his quick-thinking, we can follow. A freighter arriving on the planet also reported a close encounter with a departing ship that was not authorized to leave. Gable and Qadir are preparing a warship to go after them. Were you successful in retrieving the Heart of the Cat?" he repeated.

Walkyr shook his head. *'Follow the hunters, and you will find her,'* the

Goddess had said. "No, but I think the prisoner knows where I can find it," he quietly responded.

Vox's eyes narrowed. "Prepare to join Gable and Qadir, Walkyr. Find the Heart and bring it back," he ordered.

Walkyr nodded. "I'll leave right away," he said.

Pallu silently held out a communicator to him. Walkyr nodded his thanks and took it. The sooner he left, the faster they could intercept the ship.

"Transport on my signal," he instructed.

A moment later, his body was tingling and a wave of disorientation swept through him again. This time the feeling was caused by the reorganization of his atoms as he was beamed up to the waiting warship.

Cat's Balls, but I miss the old days when I just flew into space, he thought with a shudder.

CHAPTER FIVE

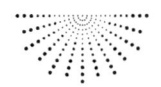

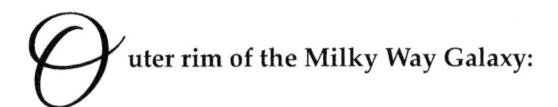

Outer rim of the Milky Way Galaxy:

The explosion shook the rebel warship, throwing Walkyr and his brother, Qadir, off balance. They were part of an elite squadron of warriors who had transported aboard the moment the shields had failed. They had overtaken most of the ship and were working their way down each level. He hoped the ship's computer system would give them information.

A curse slipped from his lips when the ship rocked again. It appeared the rebels were determined to fight to the end, if the continued explosions were any indication. He braced an arm against the wall and peered around the door leading into the flight deck. The room was filled with fighters and other assorted types of transports. Qadir looked over at him when the alarms blared, while the emergency lights started to flash.

Walkyr signaled his brother to stay back as he visually scouted the flight deck's interior from his position behind the frame of the bay door. Qadir nodded, crouched, and waited. Walkyr could see three men running toward several long-distance fighters, but they were out of range. He would leave the escaping rebels to the fighters deploying from Gable's warship.

The automatic fire extinguishing systems triggered causing a wall of smoke to rise upward when it extinguished the array of fires scattered throughout the bay. The air filtration system activated, drawing the smoke up and out. Walkyr lifted his arm to cover his nose. Through the haze, he suddenly noticed enemy combatants within firing range. Raising his weapon, he fired three shots. The flash from his laser pistol briefly lit up the flight deck. He had struck one, while Qadir followed up by striking the other two when they turned. He was about to advance when he heard a computerized voice issuing instructions.

"Self-destruct sequence has been initiated. Count down has begun. Evacuate… evacuate… evacuate," the computer's automated voice announced.

"Cat's balls, Walkyr! They are going to blow up themselves and us with them," Qadir growled.

"Not all of them," he grimly replied when a dozen ships lifted up and began a rapid escape.

"Gable, the ship is set to self-destruct. Get our men out of here," Walkyr ordered into his comlink.

"Affirmative. We are evacuating the rest of the team now," Gable instructed.

"Walkyr, to your left," Qadir suddenly said.

Walkyr rose to his feet and looked to the left. Three men had emerged out of another doorway and were striding across the deck. He immediately identified one of the men as the escaped prisoner from the medical transport. Airabus had been identified from a facial scan that had been on record from his time as an elite guard at the palace.

Walkyr's gaze moved from Airabus to the man walking next to him. The ornate cloak indicated this was probably the 'High Lord' he had been hearing about during his time in the encampment. His features were hidden in the shadow of his deep hood. The lights flickered as more explosions rattled the ship. Walkyr focused on the man's arm when he raised it to grip a support on the platform he was ascending. The lights reflected off the metal limb.

"I think we've finally found who we were searching for," Qadir replied through gritted teeth.

Walkyr nodded. They needed to track the ship in case the men were able to escape. His brother must have realized the same thing. Qadir grinned at him and pulled several disks from his utility belt. With a snap of his wrist, the disks lit up, swirled through the air, and landed in a neat line on the spaceship.

"Self-destruct in fifty-nine, fifty-eight, fifty-seven…," the computer stated, counting down.

"Gable, now would be a good time to lock onto us," Qadir urged into his comlink.

"I'm going to need a long-distance fighter as well," Walkyr added as everything blurred.

∽

Earth: Several Weeks later

Walkyr crouched down in the thick snow and watched two men working on the underbelly of a modified Sarafin transport. Dark scorch marks, deep holes, and twisted metal showed evidence that they had received some damage during their escape two months before and hadn't fared well upon entering the planet's atmosphere.

He watched and listened as the two men talked, trying to determine whether they were alone. He recognized one of the men. He had been the third man walking alongside Airabus and the elusive leader of the traitors. He didn't recognize the other, heavy-set warrior. He must have already been aboard the ship. Regardless of who they were, they needed to be stopped.

He silently advanced on the pair. It would be best to keep the element of surprise for as long as possible. Once they were eliminated, he would alert Gable to send someone. He would need assistance removing all evidence of their presence on the planet.

"I hope the High Lord and Airabus find what they are looking for. I don't like being here," the heavy-set warrior said.

"It doesn't matter what you like, Nastran. What matters is following orders. The Grand Lord will retrieve the Heart, and our people will be free to rule any world, including this one," the man from the launch bay stated.

Nastran sneered as he removed a partially ripped panel. "I've been hearing that same promise for centuries, Ranker. The only good thing that has come out of this is that we are no longer working with the Valdier," he retorted.

"I, too, prefer not to deal with the Curizan and the Valdier. They have no place in what is to come. Only the Grand Lord can free our people and give us the power of the Goddess. Once the power is ours, then even the Curizans and the Valdier will bow to us," Ranker coolly replied.

"I say we kill them all. Letting them live is too dangerous," Nastran stated.

"You need to think above killing. The High Lord has shown us what is possible once we harness the power contained inside the Heart of the Cat. The Sarafin will be the most powerful species of all. The power of the Goddess will no longer belong to just the royal family. You will see when the High Lord and Airabus return," Ranker quietly replied.

"If the power is real," Nastran snorted.

Walkyr curled his lip in disgust. These men were only interested in power, with no inkling of what it meant or how vulnerable the fate of their species truly was.

The power given to the Sarafin through the Royal line allowed them all to shape-shift. The coats of their cats were thick enough to withstand the fire of a dragon or the energy of the Curizan. Walkyr had observed enough of the Curizans over the centuries to know that it was not just their ability with technology that made them different, and Vox had grudgingly confirmed his suspicions.

What we do? his cat asked.

Walkyr smiled. *We only need one alive. I prefer the one that appears to know a little more about what is going on,* he dryly added.

His cat agreed that Nastran was the expendable one. Walkyr was about to take a step forward when he heard a machine approaching. Before he could attack, a strange transport appeared between two trees. A small figure encased in a weatherized white suit sharply jerked the steering handle on the machine to the side. Walkyr uttered a loud curse when he saw the two men reach for their weapons.

So much for the element of surprise! he thought as he sprinted forward.

He lifted his weapon and began firing. At the same time, he rushed toward the human on the machine. The two men returned fire, one aiming for him while the other targeted the human. Walkyr leaped toward the transport, wrapped his arm around the human's waist, and turned in midair. A loud hiss escaped him when he felt the searing burn of several shots striking him.

His back hit the softly packed snow, and he and the human in his arms rolled several times. He immediately shielded the human with his body and lifted his weapon again. Both men had taken refuge behind the panels they had removed. The machine the human had been riding slid to the side and disappeared between two trees.

Walkyr released the human, pressed his hand against the device on his wrist, and held out his arm. Pallu had given him new adaptive defense technology. The glow of a circular protective shield flared up in front of him, lighting up as blasts from the two men's pistols struck it. He kept low to the ground and in front of the smaller human.

"Do you understand me?" Walkyr growled, using the language Riley and Tina had taught him.

"Y…yes," the squeaky, frightened voice replied.

"You are in danger. You must get on your transport and escape. I will cover you," he instructed, lifting his arm and firing.

"Who… who are you? Is… is that a… a spaceship?" the young boy asked in an incredulous tone.

Walkyr gritted his teeth. "Yes, that is a spaceship and if you haven't noticed, we are being fired upon. I suggest that you run. I will protect you," he replied.

"Oh, okay… but, who are you?" the boy asked, still unmoving.

Walkyr grimaced when he felt the blows to the shield. A soft beep on the screen showed the power had been reduced to seventy percent—and it was dropping rapidly. If he didn't get the human out of here soon, they would both end up dead.

"I'm an alien warrior who is trying to save your life. Will you please run to your transport?" he snapped in a harsher tone than he'd intended.

The boy's eyes widened behind the yellowish tint of his goggles, and he nodded. Scrambling backwards on his hands and feet, he twisted and pushed to his feet. The boy stumbled and looked over his shoulder. Walkyr growled again at the boy to run. The shield had dropped down to thirty percent.

The moment the boy disappeared into the woods where his transport had vanished, Walkyr opened up rapid bursts of laser fire at the traitors. He holstered his pistol when the power level flashed red. Pulling a small round disk from his waist, he threw it and turned.

Walkyr took off running toward the woods after the boy, shapeshifting as he ran. The sleek body of his cat cut across the snow-covered ground. Ahead of him, he could hear the motor of the transport revving up.

He bent his head when a blast of snow hit him in the face, kicked up by the progress of the machine. The back end of the transport weaved drunkenly for a moment before the boy leaned forward and took off at a rapid pace.

The boy was a good hundred yards ahead of him when the force of the blast snapped the trees behind Walkyr and sent him tumbling over the small embankment. He rolled to his feet and shook his massive head.

A sound behind him warned him that he was not out of danger yet. Turning his head, he snarled savagely when he realized the explosion had started an avalanche. Massive amounts of snow on the steep hill began to roar down the side of the mountain.

Have to protect human child, his cat warned.

I know! Walkyr harshly replied.

He took off after the boy who had taken his warning to heart. The transport was speeding away from the scene. Walkyr needed to catch up with the boy, keep him safe, and somehow convince the human not to reveal what he had seen. This mission was becoming more hazardous with every second.

Must run faster, he told his cat.

His cat responded by spreading his toes further apart to better avoid sinking into the snow and lengthening his stride as he ran. He jumped over a fallen tree before swerving around another. The rumble behind him grew.

Hope filled him when he saw that the ground was rising. The transport ahead of him weaved back and forth, struggling to get up the steep incline. The boy looked over his shoulder as he crested the hill, then he focused ahead of him, pausing for a moment before he gunned the transport and disappeared over the other side. Walkyr lengthened his stride even more, running as fast as he could as the cascade of snow crashed to the ground behind him, showering him in a blinding tidal wave of ice, snow, and debris.

Walkyr crested the rise and looked back over his shoulder to assess whether the two men had survived. Before he registered what he was seeing, he heard a deep, blaring noise. He cursed when he realized why the boy had paused at the top of the rise. There was a road, and a massive transport was barreling toward him. His cat tensed and sprang out of the transport's path.

The large transport missed him, but the one heading in the opposite direction did not. The impact was excruciating. He rolled over the hood, smashed into the windshield, and tumbled to the ground, rolling several times before he came to a stop.

Walkyr's cat painfully struggled to stand up but fell onto his side. Walkyr lifted his head and hazily searched for the boy. He vaguely recognized the tracks from the boy's transport before the black spots blotted out too much of his vision and his mind clouded.

In the background, were the sounds of vehicle doors opening and slamming shut. The loud, excited voices of humans reached him. He knew he needed to get up. He needed to escape into the woods, but his cat's pain was overwhelming. He dared not shape-shift. He would heal faster in his cat form than in his two-legged one.

"What the hell is that? It came out of nowhere!" a deep voice exclaimed.

"I'm shocked it didn't total your truck. I've never seen a cat like that before," another voice said.

He lifted his head and opened his eyes when he felt a hand reach down to touch him. He could make out a blurry man in a uniform. The man jerked back when Walkyr's cat moved. Unable to resist the darkness that pulled him down into its greedy claws, he laid his head back down and sighed deeply.

"Is he dead?" the deep voice asked.

"No. Help me get him into the back of my truck. I'll take him to the rescue center," another male voice said.

"You work there. Do you know what kind of cat this is?" the deep-voiced man asked.

"No, but someone there is bound to," the uniformed man replied.

Pain dragged Walkyr back to consciousness a few minutes later when the men rolled him onto something smooth and dry. He winced and groaned but didn't resist. He heard the men count to three before a wave of dizziness washed through him as they lifted him into the air.

Another pain-filled moan escaped him when they gently laid him in the back of the truck. He tried to lift his head when two of the men jumped over the side of the vehicle. The slamming of the tailgate reverberated through his head, sending another shaft of pain through it. He plummeted back into the blissful insulation of darkness.

CHAPTER SIX

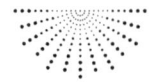

Big Cypress Reservation, Florida

Trescina grimaced as another mosquito buzzed around her. Despite the light, chilly breeze, the little blood-sucking vampires were looking for their next victim. She pulled up the hood of her windbreaker jacket and waved her hand to shoo the pest away.

It was hard to believe it was January already. Her short vacation to visit an old friend had flown by. She waved to a couple of young teens on horseback and grinned when she saw their wide eyes follow her as she carefully skirted them in order not to scare their mounts.

"How does she do that?" Joe Billie said in awe.

Josie Tiger shrugged. "Grandfather says they are her animal spirits," she replied, tapping her heels to the side of her mount.

"Why can't I have a cool animal spirit like that? My dad said mine is the old hound dog that I found eating out of the trash can," Joe complained.

Trescina chuckled and wiggled her fingers in Cinnamon's coarse hair. She looked down at the white female Siberian tiger when Cinnamon looked up at her. It was nice to be in an area where the cats could walk freely without being feared.

"Animal spirit, huh? They'd really be shocked if they knew the truth," she murmured.

Hearing a loud sneeze, she chuckled and looked down at Spice. The white male Siberian tiger appeared to be grinning.

"You know, I don't care how often I've seen this, it is still unbelievable," an amused voice informed her.

Trescina looked up. Her gaze softened when she saw Willie Johns sitting on a bench in front of the small general store his daughter and son-in-law owned. The old Seminole Indian was leaning forward on his cane, soaking up the sun. He was the reason she was here.

"Hey, Willie," Trescina greeted him with an affectionate smile.

"You have checked on the panther?" Willie asked.

She climbed the steps onto the wide porch. The two tigers bounded up the steps in one leap and trotted over to Willie for their morning scratch before padding to the end of the porch that was completely in the sun. Willie's gaze followed the two large tigers.

She nodded and sat down on the bench next to him. "Yes, the ribs that were cracked by the python's grip are healing. John said he is going to tag and release her sometime next week. She's only been on her own for a year. I think she will be a little more careful about what she messes with next time," Trescina replied with a contented sigh.

Willie raised a bushy eyebrow. "It was fortunate that you heard her cry and were able to save her, especially since it was dark out. You could have just as easily been attacked by either the python or the panther," he commented with a stern look of reproach.

"Yes," she said, not expanding on her response.

She didn't bother explaining to Willie that she was the most dangerous creature out in the Everglades. Instead, she sat back and listened to Willie as he chatted about his day. A small nagging feeling drew her attention to Spice. He was still lying down, but she could tell from his stiff posture that something was bothering him.

What is it? she asked, reaching out to the white tiger.

Spice turned to look at her. His demeanor was wary. Trescina opened herself to the Siberian tiger. With all cats, she was empathic physically and emotionally. She could also communicate telepathically in a manner similar to the way that she talked with her own cat.

The difference was the big cats couldn't speak to her the way her cat could. Instead, they communicated with her through images. At the moment, Spice was sending her a mixed message. He sensed something wasn't quite right, but couldn't actually pinpoint why.

She slowly scanned the scenic tropical foliage. The street was lined with cars. Occasionally, a car passed, slowing down to stare at the tigers before continuing on its way. Palm trees, palmettos, and pine trees dotted the landscape behind the rows of houses.

Trescina felt another wave of uneasiness wash through her. She wasn't sure if the unease originated from her or her cat this time. Her cat had been feeling edgy off and on for a while, but now it was spreading to the tigers. Trescina kept her head turned away from Willie as she reached deep inside. She had learned a long time ago to listen to her other half.

What is it? Is there a threat? she silently asked.

Yes, sense... danger, her cat fretted.

Is it anyone we've met here? Trescina asked.

Her eyes moved to two men walking toward the small general store. They were quietly talking. She knew one of the men. He was Willie's son-in-law, Thomas. The other man was Ron Belcher. He had been introduced as Thomas' best friend from college. Both men were in their late twenties, if she had to guess, and neither man had caused her to feel threatened when she met them a couple of days earlier.

No… something comes, her cat grunted, pacing back and forth inside her.

You've been saying the same thing for weeks now. Keep alert, she soothed.

Trescina jerked when her phone suddenly vibrated in her pocket. She reached for it, planning to turn it off when she noticed the name. She shot Willie an apologetic look.

"I need to take this," she said.

Willie smiled. "I need to speak with Thomas anyway," he said, slowly rising to his feet.

Willie waved to Thomas, and Trescina slid her finger across the screen of her cell phone and lifted it to her ear. She stood and walked down to Cinnamon and Spice where they were relaxing in the sun.

"This is Trescina," she greeted.

"Trescina, this is Heather at the Wyoming Wildlife Rescue Center," Heather Arnold replied.

"Hi, Heather, how are you doing?" Trescina politely responded.

"Good, thank you. Listen, I was wondering if you were near here. We have a big cat that was brought in this morning by one of our volunteers after it was injured in a car accident, and we could really use your help," Heather explained.

Trescina's gut twisted. She touched her stomach and rubbed her abdomen. Her cat was clawing at her.

"I'm not home at the moment. I'm down in the Everglades. It would take me four, maybe five days to drive out there," she said, calculating the distance from South Florida to Wyoming.

She listened as Heather spoke to someone in the background in a worried voice faintly laced with desperation. The tension inside

Trescina grew until she felt like it was an over-inflated balloon that would pop with the next breath. She refocused when Heather gave an uneasy sigh laced with worry and spoke again.

"Listen, we have permission to charter a plane for you. Can you get to the Dade-Collier Airport by… eight o'clock this evening?" Heather asked.

Trescina frowned. "I have my truck and fifth-wheel here," she started to protest when a new voice came into the conversation.

"Miss Bukov, this is Chad Morrison. I am representing the primary benefactor of the Wildlife Rescue Center," Chad introduced himself.

Trescina blinked in surprise. She knew who the primary benefactor was—Paul Grove. She had never met the man, but she had heard a lot about him and his daughter, Trisha, from the locals in the Wyoming town nearby. Many of the residents thought Paul had gone off the deep end and become a recluse when his daughter disappeared.

From the little she had pieced together from conversations and Internet searches, there was some suspicion that Trisha Grove and several other women she had been traveling with had met a grisly death at the hands of a serial killer who was never located. Some residents speculated that Paul Grove might have met the same fate after he disappeared a few years ago, while others believed the recluse theory. Personally, Trescina didn't know and didn't have the time to care. She had learned to stay out of other people's business.

"Miss Bukov, are you still there?" Chad asked, drawing her attention back to the present.

"Yes… yes, I know that Paul Grove supports the rescue center. I've had the pleasure of recommending big cats to them over the last four years and was pleased when they built their new facility near his ranch this past year. It is one of the reasons that I moved to Wyoming six months ago," Trescina admitted.

"Ah, yes. You are renting my sister's old house," Chad commented.

"Yes," Trescina answered.

It was a small, yellow house that suited Trescina well. It was remote and bordered both the Grove Ranch and the National Forest. She and the tigers could run without fear of being caught.

Trescina and Chad had never met in person. The rental had been set up by a realtor. She remembered the realtor mentioning that Sandy—at least she thought Chad's sister was named Sandy—had met a man and moved away.

"Then you understand the importance of the work the rescue center does. This injured animal is no ordinary cat. We need your skills to calm him so that we can assess how badly he is hurt. At the moment, no one can get near him," Chad explained.

Trescina pushed the hood of her jacket off of her head to rub her faintly throbbing temple.

"Why hasn't he been sedated? Surely the vet can sedate him so that he can be assessed," she suggested.

"The darts bounce off his coat," Heather said, speaking on a second line.

Trescina froze in mid-motion. "'Bounce off his coat'," she repeated.

"Trescina, I've never seen a cat like this. He's big—huge! I'd send you a photo, but… well, Chad said that for security purposes, it was best if we kept this quiet. I told him and Doc that you are the only one I know who would even have a clue about the species of this cat. You're the only hope we have to calm him down enough to help him. He's losing a lot of blood from a wound in his side. He could collapse at any moment, and I'm afraid it will be too late to save him," Heather urgently explained.

"I'll have a pilot and a private plane waiting for you," Chad said.

"I'll come… I… have two tigers with me…," she started to warn.

"I'll let the pilot know. Trust me, Mason won't be in the least bit surprised," Chad promised.

"I'll be there. You said eight o'clock, correct?" Trescina murmured.

"Yes," Chad replied.

"I'll be there," Trescina repeated.

"Thank you, Trescina. You… you aren't going to believe this big guy when you see him," Heather swore.

"I believe you," Trescina replied with a strained laugh. "I need to make a few arrangements for my truck and fifth wheel. I'll see you soon."

Trescina hung up the phone and clutched it in her hand. This was it. Somehow, she knew it. This was what her cat had told her was coming. For a moment, the fear rising inside of her felt like it would choke her.

The strange feelings had all started when she'd pulled her mother's necklace out again. For years, she had kept the pendant hidden, but six months ago, when she moved, she had removed the delicate gem from the protective box that her father had given her and polished it until it glowed. She had worn the necklace for a week—the time it took for her to move to her new home in Wyoming.

After a week, the glow of the necklace had become so bright and persistent that she feared it would attract attention. What was even stranger was she would swear it also had a faint hum to it, almost like the low pitch of a tuning fork. Unsure of what to do, she had placed it back in the metal box. Her father had made her swear to always keep the gem safe.

"Your mother said it was very special to your kind and must always be protected. You are old enough now, Trescina. I can't keep it safe the way you can. Keep it in the box. I love you, Trescina. You remind me so much of your mother."

Trescina could almost feel the soft touch of his hand as he had caressed her cheek. Her eyes burned as she remembered her father's stern warning. She didn't know if the glow and the resulting strange hum of the necklace were linked to her and her cat's feelings or not. She didn't remember the necklace glowing when her mother had worn it.

Afraid, she had hidden the box behind a loose panel in the back of her bedroom closet. Perhaps it was time for her to look at the necklace again.

Trescina drew in a deep breath and released it before she slid her phone into her pocket. The sound of footsteps behind her was a reminder that she was not alone. Turning on her heel, she forced an apologetic smile to her lips and looked over at Willie.

"I have to go. I've had an emergency call come in. Do you think you or Thomas could give me and the tigers a lift to the Dade-Collier Airport? I'll need to leave my truck and camper with you as well, if that is alright with you and Nora," she added.

"Can we use it while you're gone?" Willie asked with a twinkle in his eye.

Trescina wrapped her arm in his and grinned. "As long as you two don't do any kinky stuff in my bed, you can," she teased.

"Nothing kinky...?! This coming from a woman who sleeps with two tigers," Willie muttered with a shake of his head.

"You need to bleach your mind, old man," Trescina grimaced.

Willie chuckled. "Nora likes my unbleached mind," he retorted.

"Come on before I change my mind. Nora! I'm kidnapping your husband," she called out through the screen door.

"Just bring him back when you're finished. He promised to take me star-gazing this weekend," Nora replied from behind the counter.

"Wait until she finds out it will be in style," Trescina teased Willie.

Willie winked at her. "We like to do the kinky stuff out under the stars. The only time you can do it here in Florida is in the winter. There are too many mosquitoes otherwise. They bite my ass, and it itches for weeks," he replied with a shudder.

"That is way more information than I needed to know, Willie," she muttered with an amused chuckle.

Trescina turned to Cinnamon and Spice, but the tigers were already following her. She walked over to her truck and opened the back door. The two tigers jumped onto the back seat, each taking a side, so they could stick their heads out of the windows. She opened the driver's door, slid in, and pulled the visor down until the key dropped into her hand.

"You know that is the first place someone will look for the keys if they want to steal your truck," Willie grunted as he climbed into the passenger seat.

Trescina inserted the key into the ignition and turned it. She tossed her long curly hair back over her shoulder before she shifted the truck into drive. Then with an evil smile, she winked at Willie.

"The cats would eat them before they had a chance to put the truck into gear," she retorted with another wink.

She ignored Willie's wary gaze when he looked at the two cats lying behind him and focused on pulling out of the parking space. She would stop by her camper to grab the pack she always had ready for an emergency departure. She had learned a long time ago that sometimes she didn't have much time to plan her next move.

Her trip to the United States was supposed to let her start fresh. She had moved through most of Europe, but she had always been forced to look over her shoulder. Trescina had come here hoping to disappear into the vast forests that still dotted the country.

She glanced in the rearview mirror. A smile tugged at her lips. She had discovered the two Siberian tigers two days after her arrival in Miami. The cubs had been a mere three weeks old when she first saw them. She had gone to the local mall to shop when she saw the sign advertising that people could get their photo taken with rare white tiger cubs. Fury had swept through her when she discovered their handler had cared for them so little that they were near death.

That night, she had followed the man back to the motel where he was staying. He had left the cubs locked in a pet crate in his car. She had broken into the car and taken the cubs.

Trescina had also discovered a folder containing photos of a coat made from the pelt of the cub's mother and the listed price while she was going through the car. Sickened, she had spent months nursing the cubs and following the gruesome trail their handler had left behind. That trail had finally led her to an exclusive Miami boutique storing the horrifying coat that had been made from the pelt of the cubs' mother. She had stolen the coat that night and driven to what she thought was a remote area. That area turned out to be a spot where Willie and Nora liked to go.

In her grief, she had created a funeral pyre for the mother's remains. She had stayed in her two-legged form so she could hold and comfort the cubs as she gave their mother back to the earth. It wasn't until her cat hissed a warning that she realized that she wasn't alone. A couple out for an evening alone had come across her. Willie was a tribal police officer for the Seminoles who lived on the reservation.

She was thankful that she hadn't shape-shifted after she realized they were there. She wasn't sure she could kill a defenseless couple—not even to protect her identity. Consumed by her grief for the dead tigress and the haunting memories of her own mother's death, she had brokenly confided in Willie and Nora what she had done and why she was there. Nora had wrapped her arms around her as she sobbed out her grief while Willie had comforted the cubs. That night a deep friendship had blossomed in the face of tragedy and sorrow.

She blinked and looked over at Willie when he sighed. He was staring at her with a strange expression. She gave him an amused look before returning her attention to the road.

"What?" she finally asked when he continued his silent scrutiny of her.

"Nora and I are going to miss you. We'll take good care of your truck and camper for you, though," he finally responded with twinkling eyes and a wry grin.

Trescina shook her head in confusion. "Sometimes you drive me crazy. Star-gazing, my ass! I'm telling you again, no kinky stuff in my bed while I'm gone," she retorted with a teasing snort.

CHAPTER SEVEN

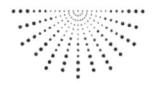

Grove Ranch, Wyoming

Early the next morning, Trescina peered out the window of the corporate jet as it landed on a wide runway. It was still dark, but thankfully the sky was clear. She could see where the runway had been cleared of the snow that had fallen overnight.

She yawned and stretched. Lifting her hands, she ran her fingers through her long, dark curls. The good thing about having such curly hair was that it always looked messy.

"Welcome to Wyoming, Ms. Bukov," Mason Andrews said.

"Thank you. I can't believe I slept most of the way," she replied with a smile.

Mason chuckled. "Luckily it was a smooth ride. Chad and my wife, Ann Marie, will be here shortly. Chad explained that you had to leave your vehicle in Florida. Ann Marie is bringing one of the ranch SUVs for you to use. We figured it would work better with the tigers and this weather," he explained.

Trescina breathed out a sigh of relief and nodded in gratitude. She had forgotten that she would be without transportation while she was here. It wasn't like there were a lot of towns with rental car companies nearby. Even if there had been, they generally didn't look kindly on having tigers in the back seat.

She motioned for the two tigers lounging between the seats to follow her. A murmur of exasperation escaped her when Spice pushed past her to stand between her and Mason who was opening the door. The tigers must have felt her cat's growing anxiety because they were doing some serious posturing at the moment.

When Spice turned to look at her, Trescina knelt down and ran her hands over his large head, then scratched him behind his ears. He rewarded her with a rumbling purr and a sandpaper lick along her wrist.

"You know I'm probably more dangerous than you and Cinnamon put together," she reminded the large cat.

She giggled softly when Cinnamon pushed her head under Trescina's arm. She pressed a kiss to the top of the female tiger's nose before doing the same to Spice. She looked up when she realized that Mason had stopped what he was doing to watch her with a bemused expression.

"I guess this must look pretty strange to you, huh?" she casually asked as she rose back to her feet.

Mason shook his head. "Maybe a few years ago, but you can trust me when I say I've seen stranger things than this," he reassured her with a mysterious smile.

She gave him a puzzled look but he just turned away to finish opening the door to the jet, and she shrugged. A shiver ran through her when a blast of frigid air swept into the warm cabin. Mason exited the jet followed by Spice.

Trescina paused in the doorway. Her gaze swept over a tall man who was talking to Mason. She recognized him as Chad Morrison. She had done a little research after she had talked to him to give herself something to do with her nervous energy.

Nothing that she had learned caused her to feel threatened. If anything, he was a model citizen. Still, the quick and intense look he gave her made her wonder if perhaps there was something missing in all the accolades that had been written about the man. Her fingers dropped to Cinnamon's head and she caressed the tiger.

"Stay alert," she cautioned before stepping out of the jet and down the stairs.

"Ms. Bukov," Chad greeted, stepping closer to grab her hand. "Thank you for coming."

"My pleasure, Mr. Morrison. I look forward to assessing the injured animal," she said.

Chad nodded and tensely glanced at Mason. "Please call me Chad. Ann Marie is in the truck. I'll be there in a moment," he said, exchanging a meaningful expression with Mason. Mason nodded and shoved his hands into his coat pockets as he ducked his head and hurried over to the truck that was idling nearby.

"You have full use of the Suburban while you're here. If there is anything that you need—and I mean anything at all—here is my number. Don't hesitate to call at any time of the day or night. My sister's old place is isolated, as you know, so if you would feel more comfortable staying closer to the ranch house, there is an apartment above the barn that you can use," he offered.

Trescina reached out and took the card from Chad's gloved fingers. She turned it over and skimmed the information before looking up at him. She searched his eyes for anything that might warn her of deception. He returned her scrutiny with a steady expression that held a hint of worry.

"What are you not telling me?" she suddenly demanded.

Chad's mouth tightened, and he glanced purposefully over at the truck before he looked up at the sky and then over the surrounding landscape. His perusal only took a few seconds, but it was suspicious as hell. His gaze returned to her face, and he nodded toward the Suburban. She lifted an eyebrow, but didn't resist when he gently cupped her elbow and guided her toward the vehicle.

He opened the back door for the two tigers before he walked around and opened the driver's door for her. She slid onto the seat. He closed the door, then walked around the vehicle to the passenger side and slid in beside her.

He shut the door before he turned to look at her again. "No sense in freezing," he casually commented, glancing at the two tigers lying in the back watching him.

"It also provides more privacy," she observed.

Chad grimaced and nodded. "Yes, it does," he replied. "Yesterday morning there was an avalanche that startled the animal in question. The animal ran into the road and was struck by a vehicle. Fortunately for it, the truck that hit it belonged to the rescue center. Shortly afterward, though, the cat woke up and Heather deemed the animal too dangerous to treat without being properly restrained. They have locked the cat in one of the observation rooms. I recognized your name when Heather mentioned you, but I wasn't aware of your special… uh… talent with large cats until yesterday."

Trescina shifted uneasily in her seat. It was hard to deny that she had a special talent with large felines when two Siberian tigers were listening to their conversation. It wasn't so much what Chad was saying that raised the hair on the back of her neck as it was the curious tone in his voice.

"I've worked with exotic cats all my life," she calmly responded.

Chad stared out of the window. It was beginning to snow again. She could tell he was trying to decide what to say next. The tension in the vehicle almost made it seem like they were doing a verbal dance, both feeling each other out without admitting anything.

"There are some things in this world that are hard to explain. Your connection to animals like the big cats is one of them, and…," his voice faded, and he shook his head.

She blinked in surprise when he suddenly opened the door to the Suburban and stepped out. He turned to look at her. His gaze was carefully shielded.

"Remember, if you need anything, don't hesitate to call that number. Mason, Ann Marie, or I will answer it," he stated before stepping back and closing the door.

Trescina watched Chad walk around the front of the vehicle and stride across the frozen ground to the truck. She shook her head in confusion before pulling on her seatbelt and adjusting the mirrors. She looked at the two tigers lying in the back. The seats had been laid down to provide room for their large bodies.

"I have no idea what that conversation was about. Do either of you?" she asked with wry amusement.

Spice opened his mouth and yawned his response to her question. Cinnamon groaned and rolled to her side. She pressed up against Spice in order to stretch out as much as she could. Both cats were done with being in small confined places for a while.

"Okay, okay. I'll drop you off at the house. I could use a shower and a change of clothes. If you promise to behave, I'll leave you there. That means no wandering off! I don't want you scaring anyone," she warned.

Spice grumbled and smacked his lips. She chuckled when Cinnamon turned her head and playfully nipped at her brother.

An hour later, she was back on the road. The two tigers were happily guarding the house, and she felt refreshed. Now, if she could only get *her* cat to settle down.

"What has you in such a tizzy?" she murmured, absently rubbing her stomach.

Something comes, her cat snarled.

Trescina groaned. *The cats patrolled the area while I was in the shower. They found nothing out of the ordinary, and there had obviously been no vehicles along this road since we left for vacation,* she pointed out.

I tell you, something coming, her cat stubbornly replied.

A smile tugged at Trescina's lips. The mental image of her cat crossing her front paws and glaring at her was too much for her tired mind. She laughed out loud.

"I believe you," she murmured with a tired sigh. "All we can do is stay alert and be ready for whatever happens."

Her cat appeared content with her response. Ever since her mother's death, she had been on constant alert. Sorrow coursed through her at the thought of her father and Katarina. The last attack on them nearly three years ago proved how dangerous it was for them to stay together. They had split up, keeping in touch once a month. The last time she had seen Katarina was two years ago.

It had been a brief and dangerous visit—at their father's funeral. His car accident had really been a murder, she and Katarina both knew it. The final police report stated that his brake line had been damaged somehow, causing him to lose control of his car and drive over the cliff. The coroner's report listed abrasions around his wrists, throat, and ankles that were not likely to be caused by a car accident, but they had not been enough to definitively label the death a murder. The investigation had gone nowhere.

Neither she nor her sister could stand the thought of not being able to claim their father's body and bury him properly. She had insisted on collecting his ashes from the funeral home. They had agreed to meet there one last time, so they could make a pilgrimage to their old home in Siberia. They wanted to spread their father's ashes among the ruins where their mother had died. That sentimental act had almost cost them their lives.

Trescina lifted a hand and wiped her damp cheek as she remembered that day. They would have both died if Katarina hadn't parked her car on a side road. A shudder ran through her, and she shook her head.

I miss you, Papa. I miss Katarina, too. One day I will find a place like Katarina did. A place where I can run without fear, she thought with conviction.

She pulled off the wide metal bracelet that she wore to cover her intricate tattoo. It had appeared shortly after her mother's death, and now it was tingling. Trescina rubbed her thumb over the delicate design before she lifted her wrist to her lips and pressed a kiss against it.

"I miss you, Mama," she murmured.

CHAPTER EIGHT

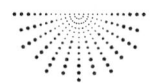

Forty-five minutes later, Trescina put her blinker on and turned onto the long driveway leading to the Wyoming Rescue Center. The unease she had been feeling the last six months had grown stronger the closer she got to the rescue center. A quick glance at the clock told her that it was still early, but she knew there was someone here twenty-four hours a day, seven days a week. Heather and her eleven year old son, Zeke, lived in a comfortable ranch-style house behind the main center. There was also a small efficiency apartment in the center itself for students or staff to stay in case of an emergency.

Trescina pulled up out front. She felt better about her early arrival when she saw the lights on in the center and someone walked past the window. She shifted the Suburban into park, turned off the vehicle, and unbuckled her seatbelt, then paused for a second before leaning over to open the glove box. She pulled out a long hunting knife in a leather sheath, then straightened in her seat and stared at the building, tightening her grip on it.

Pursing her lips in resolution, she pushed up the sleeve of her coat and sweater and fastened the sheath to her arm. She straightened her sleeves over it and pulled the knife out several times before she was confident she could get to it without any issues.

A movement at the center's window caught her attention, and she looked up to see Heather peering out at her. Trescina smoothed her sleeve one more time before she lifted the door handle and slid out of the car. As she walked forward, Heather stepped out of the building with a relieved smile a moment later.

"Trescina! Chad called a little while ago to let me know you would be on your way," Heather greeted.

Trescina returned Heather's smile. "Good morning. He mentioned that you were having trouble with an injured cat. It must be pretty serious if Chad was willing to fly me across the country," she responded.

Trescina climbed the steps and quickly cleaned the snow and mud off of her boots before she stepped inside. She waited as Heather closed the door. Reaching up, she unzipped her jacket and slipped it off. She casually folded the light brown coat over her arm to hide the bump where she had strapped the knife to her arm. She hadn't bothered with a scarf, hat, or gloves since her body temperature was warmer than normal. Of course, it didn't hurt that she enjoyed the cold weather.

Heather excitedly turned to look at her. "I've never in my life seen a cat like this. I've searched online, and I swear there is nothing like him anywhere in the world! Terry James, one of the volunteers, was so upset when he brought him in yesterday morning. He just knew he had killed him. It was a shock when the cat suddenly woke up and lunged for the door. He would have made it if we hadn't restrained him. His back leg looks like it might be broken, but I can't tell without doing an X-ray. He broke loose from his...." Heather was saying.

Trescina continued to listen to Heather explain the situation as she followed the other woman through a door and down a long corridor. Her heart sped up when she looked through the observation glass at the massive cat with black fur and an inordinately beautiful pattern of dark blue leopard spots. This was no ordinary feline. This was something else—something very, very dangerous.

Run! her cat suddenly hissed.

That was her first instinct as well. This cat was like her. She would bet her life on it. This was another shape-shifter.

Her mother had said they were the only ones. While Katarina could communicate with cats the way she could, her sister couldn't shape-shift. Her father had quietly shared with them that it was because she was half human and half shape-shifter. He explained that her mother had never told him about her past, only begged him to accept her and her infant daughter for who and what they were. He had loved them both unconditionally and kept his promise until the end to do everything he could to protect Mia and Trescina.

Trescina reached out and gripped the windowsill when a dizzying wave of memories suddenly threatened to swallow her. There had been another cat—one with a terrifying coldness in his eyes and part of his front leg missing. She could remember her mother's horrifying fear and her need to escape even as her mother tried to soothe her.

Trescina struggled to breathe when more fragmented memories returned. She remembered feeling overwhelming pain and grief. They were dying. Her mother had been mortally wounded. Then, a golden light had surrounded them, and she had been born. As she had struggled to take her first breath, she had seen the man who had betrayed her mother—the man who had hurt them.

The touch of a hand on her arm startled her. She breathed deeply and blinked as the disturbing images faded. For a few seconds, she felt lightheaded and disoriented. She shook her head to clear her mind and studied the cat through the glass. Her gaze swept over him, pausing on his front legs.

"I would like to go in… alone," she quietly said, unable to look away from the creature lying on the floor.

Heather shook her head and shot her a worried expression. "It's too dangerous. I can't sedate him. The tranquilizer darts can't penetrate his coat, and he is far stronger than any feline I've ever seen. Hell, I would put his strength on the level of a grizzly bear if I had to find a comparison," she cautioned.

Trescina suspected he was stronger than even that fierce bear, and if he was what she suspected, he would be intelligent, making him far more dangerous. She had to get Heather out of here somehow. There was no way she would endanger the woman.

She glanced at Heather. "He… won't harm me," Trescina quietly replied.

Yes, he will. Run! He one of them. He come for you. He try kill Mama, her cat hissed, clawing at her insides.

Calm down. If he is one of them, then we must kill him while he is hurt. He doesn't know who I am, which will be to our advantage. Besides, if he was one of those who tried to kill Mama, I don't think he would have hesitated to kill Heather. Until I find out who he is, you must hide so he can't sense you, Trescina insisted, pursing her lips together to keep from growling in frustration in front of Heather.

Heather bit her lip and looked through the glass into the exam room. "Are you sure? He's broken all but one of the chains holding him. I don't want to kill him, but if he attacks you, I will put a bullet through his head," she warned.

Trescina laid her hand over Heather's and squeezed it. "I will be fine. I promise," she reassured the other woman. "I'd like to do this alone. Fewer distractions will be better for both the cat and me. If you could go into the other room, I'll… I'll let you know when I'm finished."

Heather opened her mouth to protest, but closed it when she heard the chime of the front door as it opened. She reluctantly nodded in agreement before she turned and walked back to the front room.

The moment Heather disappeared, she returned her attention to the cat in the room. The large male cat was licking his injured back leg. Squaring her shoulders, she took a deep breath.

Whatever happens, don't let him sense you. We may need the element of surprise, she cautioned her cat before she turned the door handle and stepped into the room.

So much for listening to me, her cat retorted before withdrawing deeper inside her.

Oh, I'm listening to you, Trescina replied with a grim smile as she slipped her hand under her coat sleeve and pulled the knife from the sheath.

∼

Walkyr hissed in pain and frustration. His leg was killing him. For the millionth time, he cursed the mess he was currently in. It was bad enough that the boy had seen the spaceship and seen him shape-shift. He had to blow the mission by colliding with one of the humans' damn transports! To make matters worse, he needed to shape-shift to repair the damage to his body, but thanks to the camera mounted in the corner, that was impossible.

I in pain! his cat growled at him.

I know! Need I remind you that I can feel everything you do, he snapped.

Change and use healing box, his cat snarled.

In case you haven't noticed, we aren't in a place where I can do that. We have got to get out of here before I can shape-shift, and it will be easier to escape if I have three out of four working legs instead of one out of two! Walkyr retorted.

A groan of irritation rumbled through his cat. Walkyr was pretty sure his leg was fractured. If it was, he would need to access the portable medical kit on his utility belt—a nice little addition that Pallu had included before his departure. All he needed was a few minutes to use it, and he would fully heal. Unfortunately, he couldn't shape-shift here without taking a chance on being seen—and visually recorded.

He could just hear Vox if that happened! His brother would rip him a new one, as Riley would say, before turning him over to Zoran Reykill and Ha'ven Ha'darra, the leaders of the Valdier and the Curizan. The agreement had been clear between the three species—if any of them visited Earth for any reason, they were never to reveal their true identity.

Maybe Vox not find out? his cat muttered.

Did you forget they have a contact here on this world? Don't you remember the last time we visited a primitive world that didn't know there were other life forms out in the universe? Walkyr snapped.

His cat snickered. *We almost mated to purple insect,* his cat huffed before wincing in pain.

Walkyr shuddered. *With six arms and antennae,* he added.

It like me. It no like you, his cat guffawed before wincing again.

I didn't see you trying to cuddle up to it. The point is, that did not end very well. Riley and Tina have already warned us that the humans would also end up trying to kill us. Only they would do it piece by piece! Walkyr said with a shudder.

Riley try to do that to Vox anyway, his cat grunted.

Walkyr sighed. He didn't bother correcting his cat. True, Riley was always threatening to rip Vox a new one, but the truth was, his new sister adored his older brother and Vox adored her as well.

He needed to figure out a way to break free and escape. There was no guarantee that the two men back at the spaceship had died in the avalanche. He also had no idea where the Grand Lord and Airabus had disappeared to. For all he knew, they could have already found the Heart of the Cat! The only consolation he had was that their ship was buried under a ton of snow. The ship would have survived, but it would take the crew a while to tunnel through to it, and they still needed to repair the damage they had been working on before it was buried under the snow.

Find boy, too. He saw us, his cat reminded him.

I'll add him to the list of things to do before we leave—if we ever get out of here, Walkyr acerbically replied before gritting his teeth when he moved his back leg.

He was about to try working on the last lock with a sharp claw when the door handle started moving.

He turned and began to growl menacingly in warning. Shock swept through him when the guttural sound turned to a choked snort. For a second, Walkyr wondered if his cat was choking on a hairball before he realized something else was wrong with him—the damn cat was purring!

He shook his head in confusion and focused on the object of his cat's attention—the woman standing in the doorway, and immediately found himself drowning in a pair of wide hazel eyes that reminded him of the ocean, forests, desert, and stars all rolled into one. He blinked in stunned disbelief when his cat's mouth opened, and his tongue rolled out to the side like he was drunk on fermented Tiliqua wine.

Quit that! She is a human. What in the cat's balls is wrong with you? he asked in an incredulous tone.

She yummy, his cat practically hummed in a response that made absolutely no sense.

You can't eat her! Do you want to get us killed? Walkyr demanded, mentally wrestling with his cat.

Mm, eat her up, his cat purred.

Walkyr's gaze finally moved from her eyes to her lovely, riotous black curls and full lips, and then lower.... He had to admit his cat was right. She did look yummy—not that he wanted to eat her. Okay, he did, but not like that! He uttered a long string of expletives, and his body hardened when images of what his cat wanted to do to her flashed through his mind.

I don't believe this! Are you getting aroused? he demanded in astonishment.

She beautiful! his cat purred.

Yes, she was beautiful in an exotic kind of way. Her skin was the color of a sun-kissed nut while her black hair swept around her in a curtain of tight ringlets. He itched to tangle his fingers in her hair while he….

Will you stop already! Now you are making me horny, he snapped.

She coming closer, his cat happily replied, stretching his neck out to her.

It was true; she was coming closer. The woman took another step toward him, and he fervently followed her with his eyes, noting the way she casually tossed her coat to the side, the way she gripped the large knife in her hand, the way….

Knife. She has a knife. Will you listen to me! She… has… a… knife in her hand! Walkyr urgently warned his daydreaming cat.

"I think we need to have a little talk," the woman stated in a cold, hard voice that matched the look in her eyes.

CHAPTER NINE

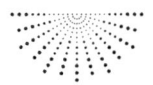

Walkyr swallowed hard when she pressed the cold tip of the very sharp knife against his throat. The woman had moved with surprising speed and agility, and given the way she was straddling his back, her foot placed so he couldn't move his good leg, the knife tip touching the artery in his neck, she clearly knew exactly where his vulnerable spot was.

She leaned forward, pressing her body against his back. "I know what you are. I will ask you two questions. I suggest you answer them truthfully or, so help me, I'll twist this knife all the way through your jugular. Do you understand me?" she murmured near his ear. She moved the knife just far enough away from his skin to allow him to answer.

Her soft, warm breath tickled the hair in his ear, making it twitch. He gave a barely perceptible nod, afraid she might carry out her threat. The boy must have told this woman what he had seen. The hole he had dug for himself was growing deeper and deeper by the minute.

"Can you shape-shift?" she asked in a harsh voice.

Walkyr reluctantly nodded. He heard her swift inhale of breath. He tensed when the knife pressed against his throat again, pricking the skin beneath his thick coat. While a Sarafin cat's fur was a natural shield to most types of blasts, it could still be pierced by a spear, arrow, or sword.

He waited to see what she would do next. "Are you alone?" she asked, slightly moving the knife away from his skin again.

Walkyr thought for a moment before he nodded again. His cat hissed at the lie. Damn cat and its infernal mood swings. Walkyr would lie to this woman if he felt like it! He didn't give a damn what his cat wanted at this moment. Between the knife at his throat and the uncomfortable hardness between his back legs, he felt like he was laying on a sword as well as being threatened by one!

You jealous, his cat sniffed.

Jealous?! When was the last time you ever got laid? Oh that's right… never! Walkyr countered.

I picky. Want mate. Not empty hole, his cat hauntingly replied. *You not to lie to mate. She get mad.*

Empty hole? Now that is crass coming from a…. Wait, what do you mean I'm not to lie to mate? Are you telling me that she is our… that she is…. Of all the Cat's balls on Sarafin, no… no… no! Walkyr's thoughts exploded into chaos.

This female—this woman—was their mate? His cat had never wanted to mate with any of the women he'd been with before. Hell, he had been lucky to have any sex at all! If it had been up to the prudish feline half of himself, he'd still be a virgin.

There had to be another explanation. His mate was supposed to be a Sarafin maiden with long yellow hair and dark eyes who would worship him. She would be sweet and gentle and… well, not like—a shudder ran through him—not like his brothers' mates. He liked Riley and Tina—as his new *sisters*. There was no way he wanted a *mate* that caused such disruption in his life.

Yes, yes, yes. Mate. No lie to mate, his cat ordered.

Technically, I gave her exactly what she asked for. She said I had to answer two questions truthfully. I did. She asked me if I understood her and if I could shape-shift. That was two questions. There is no need for her to know that there are more of us. That would only complicate this mission more than it already is, he pointed out.

Can't lie to mate, his cat stubbornly stated.

"Focus," she hissed in his ear. "I know you are talking to your cat. I want you to shape-shift so you can talk to *me*. I warn you, if you try anything, I'll shove this knife through your heart."

Walkyr lifted his nose so that it was aimed up at the camera. Out of the corner of his eye, he saw her notice what his nose was pointing to. A low curse slipped from her lips. She pulled the knife away from his neck and quickly sheathed it.

He turned his head to watch her as she got to her feet and stepped over him. Their attention shifted to the door when they heard footsteps approaching and people quietly talking in the hallway. He recognized the woman's voice but not the man's. He looked back at the woman in the room with him. She seemed as frustrated as he felt.

"Behave. I won't let you hurt anyone. Do you understand? If you try, I'll cut out your heart," she vowed.

All he could do was nod his head—and look like a total idiot because of the shit-eating grin his cat was giving her. He was going to have a very serious talk later with his primitive half. Apparently, his cat didn't understand that threatening to cut his heart out was not a sign of affection.

She perfect, his cat announced with a pleased sniff.

He watched as she took a deep breath and opened the door. On the other side, a tall man stood in the doorway beside the woman, Heather, that had ineffectually shot him with a dart yesterday. His cat uttered a guttural growl of warning. Walkyr bit back an unexpected chuckle of amusement when his newly found mate shot him an annoyed expression and gave him a pointed glare.

"How is he?" the man asked.

"Hi, Chad. He'll be alright, but I need to transport him to a different location," she said.

Heather looked shocked, but Chad was quick to respond. "It might be best to transport him to the ranch," he said.

Walkyr's cat narrowed his eyes. *Something wrong. He look at us funny,* his cat cautioned.

Walkyr had noticed the odd suspicion in the man's glances too. His concern that the boy may have told other humans what he'd seen began to grow. There were *at least* three in the know now: the bloodthirsty female his cat was in love with, the boy, and probably this anxious man too.

"My house is already located on the Grove property, so he will still technically be on the ranch," Trescina pointed out.

Walkyr's ears perked up when he heard the name Grove. Paul Grove was the father of Kelan Reykill's mate, Trisha, who was now mated to Morian Reykill, the mother of the Dragon Lords, but his residence on Earth, the Grove Ranch, was the primary contact for peaceful visitors to this planet.

How and why had this sect of *The Enlightenment* landed here? Did they know about the base and the connection to the Valdier? Once again his thoughts went back to Arrow Ha'darra. Adalard Ha'darra had been here before. In fact, he had just recently left the planet. Walkyr knew that long ago the Valdier and Curizan had worked with the traitor Ben'qumain and Lord Raffvin Reykill. Was it possible that another member of the royal Ha'darra family was working with *The Enlightenment*? He wouldn't be the first member of three royal houses to do so.

Was it possible that the Heart of the Cat had been hidden here by one of the Valdier or Curizan, and they had notified the Sarafin traitors who had then come to retrieve it? Walkyr sorted through different scenarios. He tried to remember who had been to the planet within the last year. He had just scanned a report of that information a few months ago. He knew the Valdier maintained a presence at the ranch, but he also knew that several members of the Curizan had been here, including Adalard and Bahadur, the most infamous Curizan general.

It was difficult for him to believe that any of them were a part of this, but he had learned that true deceit could be well hidden. He had to assume there were both genuine allies and traitors currently on the Grove property. His cat was absolutely sure which one his curly-haired vixen was.

"But... Trescina," Heather protested, "he might be a completely new species. His teeth, his body structure, his coloring—there is nothing like him on any Internet site that I've found."

Walkyr bit back a groan. Now there were *four* humans who knew too much, though two of them probably didn't count if they were already involved with Grove Ranch—and if this sect of *The Enlightenment* had come to Earth to meet with someone from his star system, there could be more threats than he had originally expected. This mission was getting more complicated by the moment. He would need to contact his brothers and hope they had followed him. It looked like he was going to need some assistance.

Of course, all his cat cared about was that they now knew his so-called mate's name: *Trescina*.

Trescina shook her head. "He is a rare cat found in the remote regions of Siberia. He was probably illegally purchased as a cub and brought here as a pet. They are endangered, so I know he couldn't have been legally obtained. The few that have been found outside of the remote sanctuary were all illegally taken, often at the cost of their mother's life," she explained.

"But.... Are you sure? I searched the images I could find on large cats, and I swear there wasn't any mention of a feline that looked like him," Heather repeated.

"You can't find anything about them for a reason, Heather. His kind has been hunted almost to extinction. The organization that I work with has done everything they can to keep his species alive and unknown. It is imperative that I move him to an undisclosed location. Do you know if Terry or anyone else has taken any photographs of him?" Trescina asked.

Mate good. I no even smell lie, his cat sighed.

Well, that is a great skill to have! The ability to lie and not get caught, Walkyr sarcastically responded.

"No. Terry was in such a panic that he didn't take any. Like I told you earlier, he was terrified he'd killed the poor animal and then he was worried that he'd be blamed for the damage to the truck," Heather said, lifting her hands and running them through her hair. "I swear between Terry being afraid he is going to be fired and Zeke, I'm going crazy."

"What happened with Zeke?" Chad asked.

Heather shook her head. "Nothing—yet. I caught him on the snowmobile yesterday. He was supposed to be grounded. He's eleven going on eighteen at the moment. If he isn't careful, I might not let him make it to twelve," she replied with a frustrated sigh.

"Heather, I want you to delete any video you might have of the cat, and ask Terry not to say anything…, please. If word got out… well, it could cause an international incident," Trescina added, looking over her shoulder at him with a pointed glare when he snorted at her audacity.

"What? Oh, no worries on the cameras. The system died a couple of days ago. I have a call in for the technician to come out. He's scheduled for next week. Trescina, I think his back leg is broken. I'd still like to check him over. He could have suffered additional injuries. From the damage to the truck, I have to agree with Terry about being shocked he didn't die," Heather said.

Walkyr coughed. Once he had the three humans' attention, he sniffed loudly, shook his head, and looked at the human woman who had threatened him.

Mate, not human woman, his cat disdainfully reminded him.

Whatever. As long as she understands that I will not abide the human healer's barbaric procedures, he replied, using another one of Riley's favorite sayings when Vox was on a roll about something.

"I... don't think that is necessary. I'm sure he'll be fine in a few days," Trescina reassured the other woman with a hesitant smile.

Heather looked shocked, then doubtful, and she shook her head.

"Are you sure? I swear when I called you last night he looked half dead. I can't believe he isn't in worse shape. I only had time to do a brief exam before he woke up and I couldn't knock him out again. That's when I thought of you and called. I'd still feel better if I gave him a more thorough exam before you took him," Heather insisted.

"I'll see what we can do," Trescina replied, looking at him with a calculating expression, "but I worry that his owner might try to steal him back. He is bound to know he'll be in trouble and might become violent. I'm sure the first place he will check is the rescue center. I believe I have a better chance of concealing him at the house. Once he has a chance to recover, I can make arrangements to have him returned to the sanctuary back home. I know they would love to have another male cat to help diversify the gene pool. Besides, this specific species of feline is known to be aggressive and unpredictable, and I know Heather has a full plate at the moment. He will do better in an isolated location," she added.

Chad looked cautiously relieved, and Heather nodded. "It's true that the center is full. This room is the only free space at the moment. There is also a group of high school students attending the pre-vet program tomorrow. It will be impossible to keep him hidden from them, and I know that every single one of those kids will have a cell phone on them," she reluctantly agreed.

Walkyr listened with a mixture of amusement and impatience as Trescina spun her outrageous lies. Her comments about adding him to the gene pool had almost been too much. First, she threatens to slit his throat and now she says she is going to use him for breeding purposes.

As far as he was concerned, *she* was the only one who would be participating with his *breeding purposes!*

Told you she our mate, his cat purred.

He hated to admit it, but he was afraid his cat might be right. He had been horny before, but not with this much intensity. He had never experienced an attraction this strong or swift to any female—all while he was dealing with a fractured leg and chained as well!

Mate better than empty hole, his cat stated in a dismissive tone that held just a touch of superiority and sarcasm.

Walkyr grimaced and visualized curling his fingers around his cat's throat. For a brief moment, he wished it were possible to strangle his arrogant half—especially when his cat looked up at Trescina with that shit-eating goofy grin. She must have noticed his reaction to her comment because she shot him another pointed look of exasperation. If it weren't for the fact that he was in pain, in the middle of a dangerous mission, and not supposed to reveal his identity, he would have shape-shifted right then and there just to see her try to explain it away. Once he was healed, he would teach her not to hold a knife to his throat and threaten to use him as a breeding tool!

You feel too now. Mate worth wait, his cat gleefully informed him as he stretched his front paws out and extended his claws.

It's been a while since I've been with a woman! he protested. *We've been a little busy trying to save our people! Just because I find her attractive doesn't mean I agree that she is our mate. You've been wrong before. Now behave before we get in a bigger mess than we are already in,* Walkyr growled.

I not wrong, his cat retorted with a pout.

Chad seemed to waver between wariness and hope when he looked at Walkyr's cat. "If you're sure," he finally said. "When I first saw him after he was brought in, I thought… well, we are lucky to have your expertise with exotic cats from around the world. It's good to know that he is just an unusual leopard!" he laughed uneasily, and Walkyr decided this man must be one of the genuine human allies involved with Grove Ranch. That was good to know. He wondered if all the lies were just for Heather's benefit or if there was another reason why they weren't being honest with each other. "If you are sure you can control him, then it might be best to take him to your place. I've seen the way you handle your tigers, but I think this cat should be caged—for your safety and my peace of mind. If you need help with anything, let me know," he insisted.

"I will, and I'll take you up on your offer of the cage. You're right. It might come in handy," Trescina replied with a slight smirk before her voice faded when the front door chime sounded.

"Hey, Mom, are you in here?" a young male voice called out. It was the boy from yesterday. Walkyr recognized his voice.

Heather grimaced. "I'll be right back," she sighed.

This must be Zeke. From what he could tell, the boy had not mentioned what he'd seen to his mother or Chad—yet. Once again, he wished he had been more careful. The boy's sullen tone carried from the next room as they talked. It brought back memories of his own youth. He and his brothers had given their parents more than a few reasons to growl at them.

That sense of rebellion may be why Zeke hadn't told his mother what he had seen. It was also possible that the boy thought he might have imagined what he'd seen. Their encounter had been very brief and it had happened during a period of extreme danger. As long as Trescina insisted he was some rare creature from her world, and the traitors' ship was buried, there would be no evidence to support a wild claim of aliens and shape-shifters.

"Trescina," Chad quietly said, drawing Walkyr's attention back to the man.

Walkyr growled in warning when the man touched Trescina's arm. Chad looked at him with a guarded expression. Walkyr rose to his feet, favoring his injured leg, bared his teeth, and moved his gaze from the man's face to the hand touching Trescina and then back to his face. Chad nodded warily and immediately pulled away.

"I'll be alright. I told you, this type of cat is notorious for its temperament around people. A few days of healing in a quiet place and he'll be feeling better. I'll make sure I keep him secure," she said.

Chad shook his head. "It's not that. Are you sure this… cat is what you say it is?" he asked.

Trescina turned and locked her eyes with his. She nodded. Walkyr frowned when he saw a look of fear flash through her eyes before it was gone.

"You don't need to worry, Chad. I know exactly what he is," she quietly replied.

CHAPTER TEN

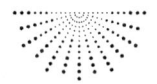

"Back off, you two. No, you can't sniff his you-know-what, Cinnamon. That is just gross. Spice, will you quit growling? He's in a cage and not going to hurt anyone," Trescina scolded.

Chad chuckled uneasily as he watched the two white tigers curiously circle the cage. He had followed Trescina from the rescue center to the quaint yellow cottage. He was glad the house couldn't talk. If it could, he was sure that Trescina's unusual pets would be the least surprising things it would share.

Sometimes Chad felt like he was lost in Alice's Wonderland. All he needed was the Queen of Hearts to come thundering out of the woods shouting *'Off with her head!'* at the top of her voice. Instead, he was helping Trescina gingerly move the cage from the back of his truck and into the attached garage.

He stood back and watched as she tenderly scolded the white tigers who were trying to assess their new visitor. Instinctively, he swept his gaze over the house that had formerly belonged to Carmen Walker and her husband, Scott. For a moment, he felt a sense of regret when he remembered the beautiful young woman who had known both love and profound tragedy during her time here. In some ways, those memories seemed as if they were from a lifetime ago instead of a few short years. It was hard to believe that Carmen—and his sister, Sandy, who had resided in the house after Carmen left—now lived on Valdier, an alien world that he could only imagine with its dragon-shifting warriors and their gold symbiot companions.

He had debated if he should mention the unusual visitors that came to the Grove Ranch to Trescina before he silently shook his head. He would if it became absolutely necessary—and he had her signature on a non-disclosure. The last thing he wanted to do was frighten her with tales of shape-shifting aliens.

He half-wondered who he was kidding as he watched Trescina scratch one Siberian tiger under the chin while pressing a kiss to the nose of the other one. Given the way she handled these wild cats, Trescina would fit right in with their alien visitors. Her ability to communicate with them was right in line with the strange things the alien warriors did. He would never forget the day he'd pulled up to the ranch and found a bunch of baby dragonlings slipping into the house and devouring the breakfast Ann Marie had made.

Lately, the alien visitors were beginning to seem more like visiting tourists and a lot less alien to him. Fortunately, there were currently none visiting the ranch. For the last couple of years, it seemed like there were almost always a handful of aliens from different worlds at the ranch.

Last month, it had reached the point that Ann Marie grumbled it was a full-time job trying to keep up with their arrivals. It was becoming harder and harder to keep their activities a secret. He and Mason were waiting for the day when the government suddenly descended on the ranch wearing radiation suits and brandishing big guns.

"I really need to retire," he muttered under his breath.

"What?" Trescina asked, turning to look at him.

Chad shook his head. "Nothing. Where do you want him?" he asked, nodding toward the sleeping leopard in the cage.

"I've got it from here. The cage is on wheels. I'll close the garage door. He'll be fine," she reassured him.

"Trescina...," he started to say, looking at the leopard with a frown.

"Is there something wrong?" she asked.

Chad shook his head again and sighed. "I hope not. I really, really hope not," he murmured. "If you need anything, let me know. I'll come by tomorrow and check on you."

Trescina hesitated a moment before she nodded and smiled at him. He sensed that she didn't really want him around. Once again, he felt a nagging suspicion that he was missing something. Perhaps it was time to pull the background check he had completed when Trescina applied to rent the house. He had read through it, but everything appeared to check out. Even Heather had vouched for Trescina, stating that when the rescue center was first opened, she had read many of the behavioral articles that Trescina had written over the years.

He waved his hand to her when she stepped into the garage and pressed the remote to close it. Only when the door was sealed did he turn back to his truck. Opening the door, he climbed into the driver's seat. He started the engine, thankful that it was still warm enough that the heat quickly filled the interior. He glanced in the rear-view mirror before he shifted the truck into drive. If he ever had any reservations that Trescina would be able to handle the huge cat, they had dissipated when he watched her through the clear glass just before they left. He hadn't been able to hear what she was saying to the massive feline, but whatever it was, the cat appeared to understand. The cat had taken the sedative tablets that Heather had given Trescina out of the palm of her hand without any resistance before he calmly did a three legged hobble down the hall behind her and into the transport cage. Five minutes later, he was sound asleep. Chad snorted as he remembered the cat's glare before his eyes closed.

"I'm glad he wasn't an alien," he chuckled, thinking that Trescina would have been in for a shock to discover her Siberian leopard could change into a man. "I bet she's never seen a cat who could do that before!"

~

Pain shot through Walkyr when he rolled onto his side. His eyes popped open and he moaned before he closed his eyes again and gritted his teeth. He felt like he'd been hit by a full-grown dragon.

He slowly opened his eyes again. His head felt like it was filled with fluff, and his leg was throbbing, reminding him that he had yet to heal the fracture. He turned his head when he heard a loud yawn. Lifting his head an inch off the thick blanket he was lying on, he looked into the wide mouth of a creature that looked a lot like a Sarafin warrior in his cat form.

"Spice, go in the house, love. I'm sure he doesn't want to see what you had for lunch. It's good to see that you're finally awake. I was worried that you died. It would have been a pain in the ass if you had. Digging a hole when the ground is frozen can be a bitch," Trescina calmly stated.

Walkyr focused and his body shimmered as he shape-shifted. Black dots danced in front of his eyes for a moment as the change jarred the break in his leg. He breathed deeply through his nose and waited for the pain to subside.

"Your… compassion is heartwarming. How long… how long was I out?" he replied in a voice edged with pain.

"A little over five hours. You know, you probably shouldn't shape-shift with a broken bone. It will only cause you more pain," she stated.

He slowly turned his head to glare at her. "And how would you know that?" he demanded.

She grinned at him. "I've read my share of paranormal romance novels. Obviously romance writers know a thing or two about shape-shifters and broken bones," she cheekily retorted.

Walkyr laid his head back against the pad and closed his eyes. "For some reason, I'm rather glad I have no idea of what you are talking about," he muttered.

She stood up and walked closer to the cage. He peered up at her through the bars. She was holding a steaming mug between her hands.

"Who are you?" she quietly asked.

Walkyr gazed up at her. "Prince Walkyr d'Rojah," he replied with a wry smile.

She looked at him with a skeptical expression. "So, is Prince your first name or a title?" she asked.

"My title. Do you think perhaps we could continue this conversation after I have healed my injuries?" he inquired.

She looked at his leg. "I had Heather X-ray it before we loaded you in the back of Chad's truck. Fortunately, you only suffered a hairline fracture of the fibula. You have really dense bones, by the way. That would explain why you are so damn heavy. We had to use the winch to get you up the ramp and into the truck," she replied.

He looked at her with a disbelieving scowl. "I can't believe you lied to me. You swore you would not let that woman near me with her primitive medical tools," he said with a shake of his head.

"No, I didn't. I promised not to let anyone hurt you if you took the sedative," she corrected.

"I only agreed because you threatened to leave me there if I didn't," he retorted.

He pulled the portable medical device from the pouch around his waist, turned it on, and switched the scanner to bone regeneration. Running it along the back of his leg, he felt immediate relief from the throbbing pain. He switched the device to tissue repair and ran the device over his calf before he moved the soothing beams over the other bruises on his shoulder, arm, and hip.

"What are you doing?" she curiously asked.

He shot her a frown. "Healing the damage from my collision with the transport," he answered.

The skeptical expression returned to her face. "With a flashlight?" she scoffed.

He shook his head in irritation. "This is not a flashlight. It is a portable medical repair unit that my brother developed," he explained, holding up the device before sliding it back into a pouch at his waist.

"Yeah, right. I see you've been watching a few too many science fiction movies when you're not out killing people," she sarcastically retorted.

"The men I was trying to kill are traitors to my world. I need to keep this situation contained. How many humans know about me?" he demanded, twisting around in the cage until he was facing the lock.

"Traitors…. Your world…. You shouldn't move! Your leg….," she stammered, backing up several steps.

He looked at her and gave her a sharp-toothed grin. "Healed. Now, will you let me out of this cage, or am I expected to get out of it myself?" he queried.

She shook her head and looked at him with wide, wary eyes. Her lips parted, then she clamped them together, and placed the cup of steaming liquid on a long shelf near the steps leading into the house.

At first he thought she was going to unlock the cage, but then she reached behind her and pulled a disturbingly familiar device out of her back pocket. He paled when he saw it and scooted to the back of the cage, far from the opening. Raising his hands in the air, he kept his gaze locked on the black box in her hand.

"Be careful with that thing. If it is what I think it is, neither my cat nor I like it. I've seen what it can do," he said.

She waved the taser at him. "Good. Then I guess you are going to answer my questions without giving me any trouble," she snapped.

"I will answer your questions if you answer mine," he countered, slowly lowering his hands.

She shook her head and gave him a grin that sent a shiver of unease down his spine. "I don't think you are in a position to negotiate. First off, I want you to remove that nice little belt you have on. Keep one hand in the air and remove it with your other hand. I'll take the weird holster at your side and the blade in your boot, too. If you try anything, I'll light you up brighter than Macy's on Christmas Day," she threatened.

"Why don't you take my clothing as well? That way you could leave me completely defenseless," he snapped.

He was surprised when he saw her cheeks turn a rosy shade of red. His irritation turned to amusement. His badass female—another phrase he'd learned from his new sisters—wasn't as bad as she pretended.

Empowered by that knowledge, he did as she asked. He threaded his utility belt through the bars of the cage before he removed his laser pistol and slid it through as well. Finally, he removed the blade he had sheathed in his left boot. He had to admit he was impressed with her thoroughness. When he was done, she carefully knelt and pulled the items out of his reach.

"Are you going to ask me questions or simply leave me guessing what you wish to know?" he asked, folding his arms and leaning back against the cage.

"Where are you from?" she demanded.

He raised an eyebrow. "Far away," he replied.

She scowled at him. "That's not an answer," she retorted with a frown.

He studied her face. His fingers itched to gently sweep a curly strand of hair back from her cheek. His body responded to the thought. This was crazy. He was sitting in an animal cage thinking that all he wanted to do was run his fingers through the soft hair of the woman who was threatening him.

That not all, his cat snickered.

Shut up, he muttered.

He leaned his head back against the bars. "My home world is called Sarafin. I could give you the specific location, but it would be easier to show you on a star chart—though, I seriously doubt your scientists are familiar with my galaxy. According to my brothers and their mates, humans are not aware that alien life truly exists," he calmly explained.

She warily stared at him, then slowly sank back down onto the steps. Behind her, he could see the white heads of two tigers. His cat purred.

What are you so happy about? he asked.

She love cats, his cat replied.

Walkyr didn't bother to point out that while she might love cats, she also hadn't hesitated to hold a knife to his cat's throat or threaten to shock him. He kept his gaze locked on her face. She was very pale, and her hands trembled.

"Are you telling me that you... that you are an alien from another planet?" she demanded.

He gave a brief nod. "Yes. The Sarafin are cat-shifters whereas the Curizans harness the energy around them, and the Valdier are dragon-shifters. Who and what we are is a gift from the Goddess," he quietly added.

He sat forward when she swayed. He warily eyed her hand when she tightened her fingers around the device. She must have sensed his worry because she aimed the taser at the ground.

"I want to know everything," she ordered in a low, quivering voice. "I want to know about your world, how you got here, and most importantly, why you are here."

"If I swear on my honor that I will not harm you, will you release me? I will tell you everything that you wish to know. I believe we would be a little more... comfortable if I was not sitting in a cage," he suggested.

Her eyes narrowed in suspicion. He tried to give her one of his most sincere, reassuring smiles. After a few seconds, his smile faded to a deep sigh when her expression didn't change. He was surprised when she suddenly rose to her feet and stepped closer to the cage.

He silently watched as she pulled a key from her pocket. She shot him a look of warning before she slid the key into the lock and twisted it. She slid the lock off, stepped back, and motioned to him.

"I swear, if you so much as breathe wrong, my cats and I will tear you to pieces," she warned.

"Don't breathe wrong or I'll be torn to pieces—yes, I understand. Your threat has me shaking in my boots," he replied, trying not to show his amusement.

She raised her eyebrow at him and gave him a sweet smile. "You should be. Make sure you shut the door behind you when you enter the house," she quipped.

He paused in mid-scoot to warily watch her. He noticed when she turned that she hadn't yet pocketed the device in her hand. She picked up the cup she had set aside a few minutes before and calmly climbed the steps into the house without a backward glance.

He had to admit he was impressed. She had just learned aliens were real and he was one of them, and already she was nonchalantly turning her back to him. That was one hell of a poker face.

CHAPTER ELEVEN

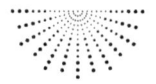

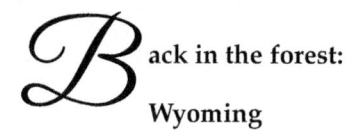

Back in the forest: Wyoming

The blanket of snow moved ever so slightly before a hand pushed up through it. A moment later, Ranker's upper body broke through the layer that had covered him. He gasped in the fresh air, pulling it deep into his starving lungs.

He struggled to pull the lower half of his body out. Shivering from the cold, he finally rolled onto the packed ice and stared up at the heavy gray clouds. He was going to kill Walkyr d'Rojah and leave him to rot on this miserable planet.

Rolling onto his hands and knees, he pushed off the ground. He looked around him. The wide gully they had landed in was half-filled with snow from the avalanche. Now the mountain above only had a thin coating of snow that had gathered overnight. There would not be an imminent second avalanche.

Ranker turned back and looked toward where Nastran and the ship should be. He lowered his hand to his side, and cursed when he realized that he had lost his laser pistol. Rolling his shoulders, he focused and shape-shifted into his cat.

What we do? his cat demanded.

We locate Nastran and the ship, and find some weapons. Then, we go after d'Rojah and the human boy, he stated.

His cat lowered its head and began to sniff. He narrowed in on Nastran's scent and began to dig. Thirty minutes later, he had uncovered Nastran's dead body. A piece of metal from the ship protruded from the man's chest. The avalanche must have thrown him onto it.

He continued digging. Several feet from Nastran's body he found the dead man's laser rifle. He scraped the ice and snow from the weapon. Checking the power, he turned and aimed it at Nastran's body. In seconds, the dead man was nothing more than a pile of black ash against the white snow.

Turning the rifle in the direction he believed the ship was located, he set the rifle to emit a wide beam to clear the area of snow. Two hours later, he had the back section of the ship exposed. He stood and carefully appraised the damage. The snow was the least of his concerns. The ship could easily rise out of the compacted ice crystals as long as the engines were clear. They would melt the surrounding snow. He would need to complete the repairs to the ship, though, if they wanted to safely escape the planet.

He strode forward and up the platform. As he entered, he tossed the depleted rifle to the side. Nastran's death was an inconvenience, but it would not affect their mission. He could repair the ship, but the first thing he had to do was warn Raul and Airabus about Walkyr d'Rojah's presence.

Ranker stepped into the small confines of the bridge. He had also lost his communicator and would have to replace it. At the moment, he wasn't sure of the other two men's location. Flipping on the communications console, he opened the channel.

"Airabus, receive," he growled, wiping his hand over his face when the snow in his hair melted and ran down his cheek.

Airabus' face appeared on the vidcom. "What is it?" he growled with annoyance.

"Have you found the Heart of the Cat yet?" he asked.

"Not yet, why?" Airabus impatiently demanded.

"You need to find it soon. Walkyr d'Rojah is here. Nastran is dead, and the ship was buried under the snow," he tersely replied into the vidcom.

The screen tilted, revealing tall trees amid a white landscape. A second later, a different face appeared. He returned Raul's icy stare.

"Where is he?" Raul demanded.

Ranker impatiently wiped at another droplet of melted snow running down his face. "I don't know. He was gone by the time I dug myself out from under the snow," he replied.

"Was he alone?" Raul coldly asked.

"We only saw him. No one else," he replied, not bothering to mention the alien child.

There was a chilly pause before Raul continued. "I want you to find his ship and destroy it. He must not have a way to get off the planet," he ordered.

"What about Walkyr?" Ranker inquired.

"Airabus and I will take care of him. Out," Raul responded.

A shiver ran through Ranker at the harsh reply. He stared at the console for a moment before he switched everything off. He couldn't help thinking that the cold, harsh voice of Raul made the snow feel warm.

He had been in the chamber when Princess Mia had refused Raul's demand to join him in ruling the Sarafin people—as well as the

Curizan and the Valdier. Instead, she had used the power of the Heart of the Cat to disappear with their newborn cub. Raul's life almost ended that night centuries ago, but his quest to harness the power of the Goddess through the gem had not.

They had barely escaped before the remaining palace guards regrouped and fought back. As they fled into the forest, an eerie, unnatural mist had descended. Since that night, they had never returned to the place they had once called home. The few who had joined them in their escape and tried to return had perished. Not even those who had once called the forest home dared to enter the malevolent woods that now seemed to be alive with an unnatural presence.

A grievously wounded Raul had ordered his followers to spread out and blend in until he called for them. The cooperation between the three royal houses of Sarafin, Curizan, and Valdier made it too dangerous to fight back just yet. Raul had gathered a small band of faithful followers and continued to covertly search for the Heart of the Cat. The only way to defeat the allied three royal houses was with the power of the Goddess.

The last few years, their search had become more and more hazardous. Raul had grown harder, colder, and crueler to those who defied or disappointed him. Many of those who had once followed Raul had drifted away, believing he was either dead or insane. Now, only a handful of his followers on Sarafin still fought and believed in what Raul had shared with them. Even Ranker had begun to question Raul's message—until they intercepted a signal that Raul prophesized would show them where the Heart of the Cat was hidden—a unique signal that had led them to this world.

Ranker curled his fingers into a fist. "We will not be denied any longer. The d'Rojah family will be the first that we destroy—then the Ha'darra followed by the Reykill. The power of the Goddess will be ours, and the Sarafin will rule over all the worlds, including this one," he quietly vowed.

He rose from his seat and looked around. Walkyr must have somehow been able to track them. He needed to search the ship and destroy any tracking devices. A slow, devious grin curved his lips.

"Perhaps I can use your technology against you. If I cannot find your ship, then I will find you," he murmured to himself.

He exited the bridge and headed for the engine room. After several minutes of searching, he located the device he had purchased from a Curizan. Now all he needed was to locate one of the tracking devices that d'Rojah must have attached to the ship. If the device did what the Curizan promised, Ranker should be able to use the signal to locate the Sarafin Prince.

"And I will take your ship for myself," he chuckled as he picked up a new laser rifle and set it on a wide beam to clear the snow around the ship.

∽

Trescina strode through the small laundry room and past the sitting room before entering the kitchen. She listened to the soft sound of the door closing as her visitor walked in behind her.

She placed her cold mug of tea in the microwave, selected the reheat button and started it. Thirty seconds later, the chime drew her attention away from the man surveying the interior of her house. She turned to retrieve her cup while making sure to keep the tall man in her peripheral vision. She pulled out the steaming mug and placed it on the counter.

"Would you like a cup of tea?" she blurted out.

He paused with a wary expression on his face. It wasn't hard to interpret what he was thinking. He was worried she might drug it. As tempting as the idea might be, she didn't currently possess any sedatives. She left that to Heather and the rescue center. She reluctantly smiled.

"That would be... nice," he finally agreed.

She placed the taser by the sink and picked up the electric kettle. She filled the kettle with fresh water and placed it back on its base. Pushing the on button, she reached up, opened the cabinet, and pulled out a mug. She blinked when she saw that he had moved to the other side of the bar.

"What… kind of tea do you like?" she mumbled, reaching for the taser and stepping back a little.

She didn't miss the way he stiffened—or the way he forced himself to relax. She watched as he placed both hands flat on the bar before he slid onto one of the bar seats. The click of the electric kettle sounded loud in the quiet room.

"I'll let you choose. I'm not familiar with the plants on this world. Riley said it might be advantageous for me to eat certain types of mushrooms or a five-leaf plant called marijuana while I was here to help me chill out. I am still trying to understand how a fungus or leaf can cause my body to become cold," he stated with a perplexed expression.

She tried to stifle a giggle which caused it to sound more like a snort. She shook her head at him and reached for the canister of peppermint green tea. Her amusement grew when he leaned forward to curiously watch what she was doing. She carefully placed the hot mug of tea on the bar before she stepped back and picked up her own cup.

"Well, you'll have to settle for something a little less… calming," she informed him before she studied his face. "You have spots."

He looked at her with a startled expression before he shrugged. "That is not unusual. Most Sarafin retain the markings of their cat in this form," he said.

"You said that you came from another… planet. Tell me about it," she encouraged.

"First, I need to know how many people the boy told about my presence," he stated in a serious tone.

Trescina frowned. "Boy? Which boy...? Do you mean Zeke?" she cautiously asked.

He impatiently nodded and waved one of his hands. "Yes. He must have told you that he saw me shape-shift. That is how you knew about me. From his mother's reaction, I do not believe he has told her yet. I am not sure if he told the human male. I sensed that *he* was unsure. Perhaps he did, but the male did not believe the boy's wild tales. If that is the case, why would *you*?" he demanded.

Trescina's mind raced as she tried to understand everything he was admitting. He thought that Zeke had told her that he was a shape-shifter. That meant that Zeke must have seen him when he snuck out yesterday. From the little that she had noticed, she thought Zeke must have not shared the story of his wild adventure. If he had, either Heather or Chad would have mentioned it. Granted, Chad had been hesitant about her taking Walkyr, but that was mostly because he was only relying on the little he knew of her and her work with large cats. It was obvious both Heather and Chad had believed her tale of Walkyr being a rare Siberian cat.

"I don't think Zeke told anyone... else. He didn't tell anyone about seeing you shape-shifting—except me, of course. I tend to believe the more... unusual things in life. It's one of my quirky habits," she hastily added.

The frown on Walkyr's face relaxed, and he nodded in satisfaction. "It is best if neither he nor you tell anyone of my presence. Both Riley and Tina were very adamant that no other humans should be aware of my presence because they would panic," he stressed.

Trescina nodded in agreement before she frowned. "Who are Riley and Tina?" she asked.

Walkyr looked over the rim of his mug. She could see his nose move as he tried to sniff the drink without being obvious. He crinkled his nose at the strong peppermint scent and looked warily at the almost clear, steaming liquid.

"They are my new sisters. Riley is mated to my brother, Vox, while her sister, Tina, is mated to my brother, Viper. Pearl, their grandmother, is married to Asim. He is a Valdier. The three women come from your world, though my brother, Vox, met Riley on the Antrox mining station he was imprisoned in," he explained, still unsure of the drink she had handed him.

She released an impatient sigh. "Let me," she said.

She placed her cup down on the counter and reached for his mug. He paused for a moment before he handed his drink to her. She lifted it to her lips, gently blew to cool it a little, before taking a sip. She repeated her actions once more for good measure before handing him the mug again.

"Why did you do that?" he questioned.

She lifted an inquiring eyebrow at him. "I wanted to show you that it is perfectly safe to drink," she stated.

"Thank you," he murmured, before turning the mug and placing his lips on the spot where hers had been.

She followed the movement with her eyes. A shiver ran through her at the romantic, almost intimate act. She swallowed and began to wonder if she might have been better off just dumping him somewhere far away.

"You were going to tell me about your planet. How did you get here? You said there were others, only you were fighting them. What happened to them?" she asked, leaning against the counter.

We in danger and you flirt with him! her cat huffed.

He is like us. We need to know, she argued.

No, we don't, her cat snorted before withdrawing again.

"You do not have to worry. I promise I am not here to harm you or any other human," he asserted.

Trescina blinked, trying to follow what he was saying. It took a second for her to realize he was studying her hands. She looked down and grimaced. Her knuckles were almost white from her grip on the mug. She was lucky she hadn't crushed the blasted thing.

"I'm not worried, and I'm definitely not afraid," she lied.

His lips twitched at her obvious fib. "In that case, I better answer your questions, since you are not alarmed. My home world is called Sarafin. We are a species gifted by the Goddess Aikaterina with the ability to shape-shift into the powerful form of a feline. Our cat is a part of our primitive side. I have the power of the leopard. My skills as a warrior match those of my leopard," he stated.

She tilted her head and studied him. "What are your skills?" she asked.

He grinned. "Power, stealth, cunning, and I'm an excellent lover," he added.

"Really? I'm sure that goes over well on your resume," she teased.

"I am not sure what a resume is, but Pearl once said that I was full of shit. She has a very colorful vocabulary. I have learned a lot from her," he replied.

His sheepish grin made her chuckle and filled her with warmth. She pulled her eyes away from his. He could add 'very good at distracting' to his list of accomplishments as well.

She cleared her throat. "So, everything you've said so far sounds pretty unbelievable. I mean, I know the shape-shifting part is true. I've seen you do it. The thing you used to heal your leg is pretty awesome too, so I'll give you the alien technology part. The other items you listed—well, I'll wait to see if those are true as well. After all, if you are so cunning and stealthy, I'm not sure jumping in front of a truck was a good demonstration of that," she observed a bit sarcastically.

His expression sobered. "I was trying to protect the boy. I have to find out if those men I was tracking were killed in the explosion. It is possible they weren't. They know about the boy and will kill anyone they come across. These are traitors to my people. They are responsible for many atrocities over the centuries. It is important that I make sure they either died or stop them before they harm anyone else," he quietly explained.

Trescina looked over his shoulder and out the windows at the forest and mountains. The area was pretty remote. It was a thirty-mile drive into town. The majority of the land belonged to Paul Grove. She looked back at him.

"Why would they come here? I mean, why come so far across space to land here? I would think there would have been planets closer to yours where they could have escaped," she reasoned.

Walkyr turned and slipped off the stool. He walked over to the window that looked out over the mountains. A light snow was falling.

She had an insane impulse to walk over behind him, wrap her arms around his waist, and hold him close. It was crazy to even think such a thing. If everything he was saying was true, then she couldn't help wondering if the faint memories that had haunted her all her life were actually real.

Are we aliens? Papa said that Katarina couldn't shape-shift because she was half human. That Mama had never changed him because it would have been too dangerous. I always thought it was because we were a different species native to this planet. But, is it possible we are not? she silently wondered.

I remember pain, her cat stubbornly stated.

Trescina straightened when he turned. His face was hard—distant. This was a man used to fighting. Yet, even with the change in him, she did not feel threatened.

"There must have been a reason they came here, to this exact location. Whatever brought them here, I need to find it first—or at least prevent them from leaving the planet. I have to return to the location where I was struck. Their space ship was not far from it. From there, I can determine if the two men survived before I track the other two on this planet," he said.

"I could take you," she volunteered before wincing at her cat's rebellion.

"I do not want to put you in danger," he started to say.

"I don't think you need to worry about that. I come with my own security force," she reassured him.

He turned to look in the direction that she waved. Trescina chuckled at his baffled expression as he studied the two tigers lounging on the rug by the thick, double-paned doors. Cinnamon was lying on her side while Spice was sprawled out with his back legs stretched out behind him. Spice looked up and yawned.

"Is it normal for humans to have such pets?" he asked in a suddenly puzzled voice.

Trescina laughed. "No, but then, I'm not your typical human," she teased. "Come on, space man."

CHAPTER TWELVE

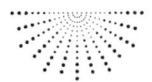

Walkyr surreptitiously studied the woman driving the vehicle. There was something about her that continued to perplex him. It didn't help that all he could think about was burying his hands in her hair and pulling her close. Those long curls were driving him crazy.

She make beautiful tiger, his cat purred.

We are not here for a mate. We are here to save our people, he reminded his cat.

We do both, his cat stubbornly argued

Walkyr shielded his thoughts. He wasn't about to get into an argument with his cat. That usually didn't end well, because one of them had to lose. His cat was known to pout for weeks and cause disruptions when he least expected it. His theory was that the Goddess had a wicked sense of humor because the Valdier had the same issues, only in duplicate except theirs were twice as bad, since they had to deal with their dragon as well as their symbiot.

He shuddered. He couldn't imagine not having another voice in his head all the time. For a brief second, he was almost envious of the Curizan. They must have it easy compared to their shape-shifting allies!

"What?" Trescina asked, glancing at him as she navigated the icy driveway leading away from her home.

He shot her an apologetic look. "I was thinking," he replied.

She looked at him with an amused expression. "So, you can add talking to yourself as another fine quality to your resume?" she teased.

"What is this resume that you talk about? Is it a disease?" he asked.

"No, it's not a disease. It is a document citing your qualifications when you are looking for a job," she explained, slowing to a stop before looking both ways.

"I do not need to look for a job. I am a Prince. My position is to protect my people," he answered with a wave of his hand.

"Oh, I forgot. You're a Prince. Of course you already have a job," she muttered under her breath. "So, killing people is part of your Princely duties I take it."

"Yes, when they are responsible for the deaths of thousands of my people, including members of my extended family," he replied.

"I'm so sorry. I… how?" she asked with horror.

Walkyr nodded and stared moodily out of the windshield. "They joined together with traitors to the Curizan and Valdier. A sect known as *The Enlightenment* recruited followers throughout the different Kingdoms on our world and others. Their lies and deceptions were effective. The Great War between our three species raged for centuries, leaving a long line of death and destruction in its wake. During a battle, two members of the Royal Families, one from the Valdier, the other from the Curizan, became separated from their parties and found themselves face-to-face." He shook his head. "It would appear the Goddess must have decided that since we refused to talk, we needed a little help. Creon Reykill of the Valdier and Ha'ven Ha'darra of the Curizan did just that. They eventually understood the depth of the treachery and reached out to my brother, Vox. A trap was set and sprung. It revealed that the extent of the perfidy which had not only infiltrated the three planets but also the Sarafin royal family itself. The members of the sect must have realized they were about to be revealed. On that same night, they planned and launched coordinated attacks on all three worlds. Their goal was to murder the members of all three royal families and seize control," he explained before growing quiet as he remembered that night so long ago.

"But… you were able to stop them! I mean, you wouldn't be here otherwise, would you?" she protested.

He nodded. "Yes, we stopped them, but not before there was a great loss of life throughout each of our worlds. The Valdier King was killed. They discovered quite recently that his own brother murdered him. The Curizan also suffered devastating losses while we…." He paused and drew in a deep breath. "The Kingdom of the Desert and the Forest on my world were devastated by the murders of their leaders. You must understand that the families rule our worlds because we were chosen by the Goddess to be the protectors for our people. All Sarafin were given a gift—the gift that gives us the power to connect with our cat. Without that power, we would no longer exist. The Prince of the Desert Kingdom was smuggled away by his nurse after the murder of his parents and brought to his aunt and uncle for his safety. Banu and I were raised together, and we are as close as brothers. He still searches for the Kingdom that belongs to him," Walkyr said, reaching up to scratch Cinnamon's chin after the white tiger rested it on his shoulder.

"What about the other Kingdom, the one in the forest? What happened to it?" Trescina asked, lifting a hand to push her hair behind her ear.

He turned his head and looked at her. "I've seen the Kingdom of the Forest. The Goddess showed me the way. I do not understand why she chose me, but she did. Princess Mia and her newborn child vanished from their Kingdom that night. The Goddess showed me what happened. Princess Mia held the Heart of the Cat, the lifeblood of our species, in her hand when she disappeared. She and her newborn child must be alive. My mission is to find them and retrieve the Heart," he quietly shared.

Trescina shook her head. "It can't.... I don't understand. How could this...? Princess Mia.... She would have to be centuries old if this happened then. There is no way! She...." her voice faded away and she shook her head again.

He shrugged. "The Goddess said the past had caught up with the present. The Goddess is not limited to the physics of time and space the way we are. I concluded that she could only mean one thing... in order to protect Princess Mia and her child, she had sent them into the future, which is now our present," he stated.

∽

Ranker held up the scanner and cursed. The Curizan's technology was not as good as he had boasted. If he hadn't already killed the man, he would have done it when he returned just for having wasted his time.

He paused and looked around. Perhaps the tracking device he had found on the outer section of the hull was damaged. He swiveled on his heel and reached for his laser pistol when he saw a movement out of the corner of his eye.

A look of disgust crossed his face when he saw a large brown beast staring at him. He straightened and lowered his arm when the creature turned his head and began to forage along the ground. He looked up when he heard a sound above him.

He climbed a steep hill. When he reached the top, a railing with a wide road was on the other side. He narrowed his gaze when he saw a gap on the other side of the road and tracks that matched that of the transport the human child was riding. A smile curved his lips. Perhaps all that was necessary to locate Walkyr d'Rojah was a little bait—human bait.

He waited until the roadway was clear before climbing over the railing and jogging across the pavement. Once the trees on the other side shielded him, he pocketed the defective reverse-tracking device and gripped his pistol. Setting off into the woods, he focused on following the deep ruts that had been left behind—tracks that he hoped would lead him to his prey.

∽

Trescina remained quiet as she drove down the road. She kept her eyes on the pavement, looking for clues on where Walkyr was hit by the vehicle. They didn't have much time to find the place. It was already starting to get dark and the snow that had finally stopped falling was threatening to start up again.

In her mind, she was replaying every word he had spoken. She had to force herself not to pull over to the side of the road and kick him out of the SUV, so she could run like hell. It was a good thing she was gripping the steering wheel, otherwise he would have seen the trembling in her hands.

We run, her cat pleaded.

No. Not yet. I need… we need to know more. He spoke of Mama. He said the Goddess showed him what happened, she replied in a numb voice.

He see because he there! her cat argued.

She started to shake her head but stopped herself in time. She wasn't in the mood to argue with her cat. If Walkyr was telling the truth—and she believed he was—then she needed to know more about the world her mother had come from and about the man who haunted her memories.

She could sense Walkyr studying her. She glanced at him. He had a frown on his face.

"What?" she demanded, beginning to feel uneasy.

"Why do you wear powder on your face? You are beautiful without it," he inquired.

She relaxed. The question was unexpected but thankfully not the one she was expecting. She shrugged. "A lot of women today wear make-up. I have a skin condition that I'm self-conscious about. I don't like it when people stare at me," she commented before she reached up and pulled her hair forward a bit more to hide the marks on her skin.

"You should never be self-conscious. You are beautiful the way you are and have no need to answer to anyone," he declared with a slight growl in his voice.

She chuckled and shot him an amused look. "Easy, big guy. I didn't say I felt like I needed to answer to anyone, and I really don't give a damn if someone thinks I'm beautiful or not. I just don't like strangers asking me questions. I have a hard enough time dealing with people in general," she calmly stated.

"Why?" he asked, confused.

She slowed the truck and turned on her blinker when she saw a set of skid marks and pieces of what looked like a plastic turn signal cover along the edge of the road. She pulled onto the wide shoulder and brought the transport to a stop. She shifted the gear into park and turned to look at him.

"Because I like cats better than people. They don't ask me questions about why I wear make-up," she replied before turning off the engine and unbuckling her seatbelt. She pushed open the driver's door after she made sure there were no vehicles approaching. "We're here."

"I thought you did not know where I was hit," he said, hastily releasing his seatbelt and opening the passenger door.

She walked around to the back of the Suburban and opened the hatch. Stepping back, she motioned for the two tigers to exit. By the time she closed the door and locked the vehicle, he was waiting with an expectant expression on his face.

Trescina released a long sigh. "It wasn't hard to figure out that this must be the place. If you look at the road, you can see the skid marks on both sides. Add the broken turn signal and the rocks with only a light coating of snow and it seemed pretty conclusive. I'm a pro at the game of Clue, by the way. It was always one of my favorites growing up. If you doubt me, check my resume under awards for World Champion Clue Gold Medalist," she cheekily concluded.

She tossed her hair over her shoulder and looked both ways to make sure the road was clear. She and the two tigers hurried across to the other side. She peered over the railing.

"Are you coming? It will be dark soon, and it feels like it is going to start snowing again," she called to him.

Trescina watched as he jogged across the road. She ran her gaze appreciatively over him. The grace and power in his stride was impossible to miss. This was a man who excelled at running, and she suspected hunting as well. A shiver ran through her that had nothing to do with the chill in the air and everything to do with the fact that she was playing a dangerous game with a man that she knew very little about. If it were not for her hunger to know more about her mother's past, she would have bolted already.

It still wouldn't hurt to have an exit strategy, she silently thought.

For once, her cat purred in agreement. She swallowed when he stepped over the railing and held her hand to help steady her as she did the same. She instinctively wrapped her fingers around his warm ones.

This was the first time they had touched, at least while he was on two feet. Her heart pounded in her chest as she stared up at him. She wasn't sure if it was because she was afraid or because she wanted him to kiss her. She forced her gaze away when she saw a flare of awareness in his eyes.

She wasn't playing with fire. She was messing with a freaking supernova! At least that was what it felt like at the moment.

Walkyr gripped Trescina's hand and slowly descended the steep terrain. He tried to pick out the easiest path, stopping several times to wrap his arm around her waist and lift her over a log or steady her when they encountered a steep drop.

"I can do this," she said in exasperation after the third time he paused.

He met her irritated protest with a wry grin. "But if you did this unaided, then I could not add being a gallant warrior to my resume. I need something to counter balance your award for the game you enjoy," he replied.

"Clue… the game is called… Clue. You have to figure out who murdered someone, the weapon they used, and the location where they did it," she said.

He gazed down at her before slowly sliding his arm around her waist again and lifting her. She gripped his shoulders. He could feel her fingers curl against his shirt as he lowered her to the ground.

"It sounds like an exciting game," he remarked.

"It… can… be," she murmured. "You…."

She gasped when she was suddenly pushed into him. A fiery blush appeared on her cheeks. She lifted her hand and scratched Spice under his chin. Walkyr grinned at the male tiger and winked. It hadn't taken much of a mental push to encourage the Siberian to come up behind Trescina. The big cat had nudged her between the shoulder blades.

He tightened his arms around her waist and held her against his body. She started to glare at the cat before she looked at him with a raised eyebrow. He grinned unabashedly at her.

"That was sneaky," she chided.

"It was worth it," he admitted.

He threaded his fingers through her hair. It was as soft as he thought it would be. He carefully studied her face. Confusion swept through him when he noticed another dark mark on her cheek. It looked almost like one of the stripes on the tigers. He released her hair and started to touch the mark when she suddenly pushed him away.

"It will be dark soon. If you want to find anything, you'll need to do it in the next half hour or so. Once the sun goes down, the temperature will really drop, and then it will be too dangerous to stay outside very long," she warned him.

Walkyr released her and turned as she walked around him. He watched as she walked along the bottom of the slope. She paused several yards down and looked up. The ground wasn't as steep and there was a gap in the railing on the top. He shook his head and lifted a hand to scratch Spice's chin. "Thank you, my friend. That brief moment of holding her in my arms was delightful," he murmured.

He chuckled when the tiger looked at him and released a small sneeze before jumping down to follow his mistress. He slowly followed with Cinnamon by his side. He tightened his jaw and reached for his weapon when he saw what she was staring at.

"The tracks from the boy's transport," he said, scanning the ruts in the snow.

She nodded. "Heather would ring Zeke's neck if she knew he had gone this far from home and crossed the highway. He's lucky he made it down this slope. Anywhere else and he could have flipped the snowmobile. There are two sets of footprints in the snow. One must have been yours, but that doesn't explain the other ones," she observed. She carefully studied the surrounding area.

"At least one of the men survived, possibly both. I need to return to the location of their ship," he grimly replied.

"It will be dark soon," she protested, looking up at the sky.

He lifted his hand and touched her cheek. "Cats can see incredibly well in the dark," he reminded her.

She grimaced. "I can go with you," she offered.

Walkyr shook his head. "No! These men are trained assassins. I will go alone. I want you to return to your home," he softly ordered.

"I'm not going to just leave you here. You don't know for sure that those men even survived. If you won't let me go with you, the least I can do is wait for you in the Suburban. You should also take Cinnamon and Spice with you. They will know what to do, and they can help watch your back," she stubbornly asserted.

He lifted his hand again and caressed her face from her temple down to her chin. "I am curious, why did you name those two cats such unusual names?" he asked with a rueful smile.

"I guess you'll just have to come back so I can tell you," she retorted before biting her lower lip.

He wanted to protest that he wanted the cats to stay with her so that he knew she would be protected. Something told him if he tried to insist, she would just do what she wanted to do anyway. He decided that she was stubborn enough to ignore his orders if he didn't compromise. He also had the feeling that he better get used to doing that. His life was going to end up being as exciting as his older brothers'.

This is what happens when your mate is a human, he informed his cat.

His cat's snickering told him that his other half was perfectly content with the idea of leading an exciting life. All Walkyr could think of was that his idea of a perfect, delicate little mate was a woman who was happy to have him home on rare occasions. He had only known Trescina a few hours, and he could not picture her contently waiting for him to return from a mission. He would be lucky if she were not the one leading it!

He released a frustrated breath. "Very well. I will take Spice, but Cinnamon will stay with you in the transport. If anything happens, I will send Spice back to you. If he returns alone, you must promise me that you will immediately leave the area," he insisted.

She pursed her lips before she nodded. "I promise," she reluctantly agreed.

He bent his head and paused with his lips a breath away from hers. He waited to see if she would pull away. When she didn't, he brushed a kiss against her lips.

"I will return," he promised.

CHAPTER THIRTEEN

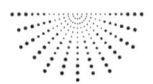

Walkyr took a step away from her. They stared into each other's eyes for a moment before he turned away. With a snap of his fingers, Spice rushed to his side. Trescina watched as they disappeared into the woods.

She lifted a trembling hand to her lips. They still tingled with the feel of his warm mouth. She was in serious trouble.

It too late, her cat quietly mewed.

What do you mean? she asked.

Her cat sighed. *You know. I know,* her cat replied.

"Yes, I know," Trescina whispered.

She lowered her hand when Cinnamon brushed up against her. She slowly knelt and wrapped her arms around the tiger, closing her eyes and turning her face into Cinnamon's soft neck. For a brief moment, she relived the memory of when she had held her mother in exactly the same way.

Tears burned the back of her eyes. There was so many things her mother never had the chance to tell her and Katarina. She had escaped death on her own world only to have her life taken on a distant one.

A sob caught in her throat. She opened her eyes and rose to her feet. A soft, watery smile curved her lips when Cinnamon nudged her hand.

"I know," she murmured.

She started to turn when she looked at the footprints again. There was only one set of tracks leading upward. There were none leading back down. If one of the men had survived, he had been following Walkyr's tracks.

"Come on. Let's see if we can find out where he went," she murmured to the tigress.

Cinnamon snorted and looked back toward the woods. Trescina sent the tigress an image of the footprints. Cinnamon turned her head and lowered her nose to the ground. She sniffed at one of the imprints before she slowly began to climb back up the incline to the road.

Together, they crossed the highway. Trescina paused by the SUV. She looked back in the direction that Walkyr and Spice had taken. She pursed her lips before she followed Cinnamon. Sure enough, the footprints followed the tracks left by Zeke's snowmobile.

"He is following Zeke," she whispered, her throat tightening with fear.

Trescina stopped. She was undecided about what to do. Walkyr had said there were two men. Perhaps one had stayed at their spaceship while the other followed Zeke. There was no way she could contact Walkyr. She looked toward the path leading into the woods. There was no telling how long ago the man had passed through the area. The fastest way to Heather's place was by road, not cross-country. The snow and unfamiliar terrain would slow down the traitor.

Turning in Cinnamon's direction, she whistled. The tigress bounded back to her. She unlocked the SUV and opened the back door. Cinnamon jumped in the back seat. Closing the door, Trescina hurried around to the driver's side. She opened the door and slipped inside. Minutes later, she pulled onto the highway and pressed down on the accelerator. All she could do was hope that Walkyr and Spice would be safe.

∼

Walkyr advanced through the darkening forest. His gaze moved from the footprints to the surrounding area. He searched for any hint of movement. Spice had moved several yards to his left. The tiger's coat helped it blend in with the snow-covered terrain.

His pace slowed as he neared the area where he knew the ship had been. Spice crouched down and stared intently at the cleared area when he stopped. Walkyr surveyed the area with growing unease.

It was obvious that at least one of the men had survived. He turned and sent an image to Spice. The tiger looked at him before silently rising to his feet and disappearing.

So far, he'd only seen one set of tracks leading away from the ship and none leading toward it. He wanted to make sure that Airabus and the High Lord had not returned to this area. Dealing with two men was dangerous enough. Confronting four could be suicide if he wasn't prepared. Spice would patrol the perimeter and alert him to any footprints—cat or two-legged.

He glanced up at the sky. The sun had set, but there was still a slight glow behind the mountains. Stars were beginning to appear between the thick, dark clouds. The temperature was rapidly dropping. Trescina had been right—there would be more snow tonight.

He turned his head when Spice emerged from the darkness. The tiger came up to him and rested his cold nose against his arm. Images flashed through the tiger's mind. Small prints along with the image of a long-eared furry creature and the fresh tracks of a large brown beast flashed through his mind.

Walkyr lifted a hand and scratched the tiger to show appreciation for its help. Standing, he slowly emerged from the trees. The area was silent except for the sound of the wind and the creaking of the trees as they swayed. The snow around the ship was littered with footprints. It looked like they were all the same size. A large area surrounding the ship had been cleared of snow creating a deep depression. The patterns on the snow indicated a laser rifle was used.

He moved forward and peered down into the hole. At the bottom, he could see the dark gray hull of the spaceship he had been tracking. The back of the ship was closed.

He scanned the area before motioning Spice to keep watch. The tiger backed up, turned and moved to settle down next to a large mound of snow. Once he lay down and was motionless, he blended in with his surroundings.

Walkyr refocused on the ship. He carefully descended into the depression. On each side, walls of ice towered above him. He soothed his restless cat.

I don't like this either, he admitted.

If any men suddenly appeared, especially from the ship and at the top of the icy walls, he would be defenseless. He paused halfway down when he saw dark ash mixed in with the snow. It was the size and shape that made him curious.

He walked over to examine it. Glancing around to make sure everything was still quiet, he pulled the medical device Pallu had given him from his utility belt. He lifted the scanner and ran it over a section of the ash before looking at the readings.

It looks like I can cross off one traitorous bastard from the list, he silently thought with a small measure of satisfaction.

He replaced the medical device and studied the closed rear door. It had been open when he had tossed the explosive. He continued toward the ship, carefully scanning the area to make sure there were no explosives set. He was almost to the bottom when his cat hissed out a warning.

Crouching, he saw the thin wire that was almost invisible in the darkness. His cat had sensed the electrical charge. He looked to the right and saw a small probe sticking out of the ice. The snow had melted and turned to ice. A quick look to the left revealed the other end.

He studied the area, paying close attention to the ground and the walls of ice on each side of the cleared entrance for additional wires leading up to the ship. He could not see or sense any other traps. Rising to his feet, he felt certain that there was no one else here. The footprints had led away from the area, and he'd found no evidence that anyone else had returned. The ash proved that one of the men died and one survived. Now the question was, where did the other traitor go?

Walkyr's expression tightened when he thought of the footprints on the side of the hill. He'd left Trescina. What if the traitor had been hiding, and he didn't sense him?

A rush of adrenaline hit Walkyr. He holstered his pistol and shape-shifted even before he had completely turned around. With long strides, he dug his claws into the snow and raced out of the depression. With a swift thought, he directed Spice to follow him. The large tiger was already in motion, understanding his fear for the safety of his mistress.

Walkyr caught up with Spice just as the tiger was entering the woods. They sped through the darkness like two ghostly creatures from a horror story, dodging trees and fallen debris that created obstacles as they flew across the snow-laden landscape.

He pulled ahead as they emerged from the woods. Turning to the right, he followed the trail the snowmobile had made. This time when he reached the top, he paused in the gap of the railing and made sure the path was clear before darting across the road.

His heart hammered in his chest when he reached the other side. In silent desperation, he looked back and forth for Trescina's transport. Nothing but empty road greeted him.

He turned his attention to Spice when the tiger moved past him and down along the side of the road where Zeke had continued into the woods. Walkyr followed the tiger. The keen eye of his cat had already made out the footprints of the traitor he had been tracking on the other side, but there was also the smaller imprint of a woman's boots and the paw prints of a tiger. He followed the tracks a short distance into the woods. The tracks of the traitor continued, but Trescina and Cinnamon's had stopped and turned back toward the road. The only thing Walkyr could conclude was that Trescina might have guessed where the man was going and returned to her transport.

A flash of the rescue center appeared in his mind. Walkyr turned and looked at Spice. The tiger was staring into the woods. The traitor was following the tracks that Zeke had left behind.

Walkyr released a savage snarl. Heather and her boy were in danger. Trescina would have pieced the clues together. She had gone to warn them. The problem was neither one of them knew how much of a head start the traitor had before they arrived. It wouldn't matter. His mate—and he accepted that Trescina was his mate—was in danger and so were the woman and her young son.

He took off running. He would follow Zeke's trail. Spice ran beside him. He matched his pace with the young tiger, knowing that he could have easily left Spice behind. He also knew deep down that he had already endangered enough lives without abandoning the tiger as well.

Soft, fat flakes of snow began to fall around them. With the Goddess' luck, perhaps the traitor wasn't too far ahead of them, and the snow would slow the man down. He refused to think of what the alternative might be.

CHAPTER FOURTEEN

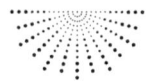

Ranker circled the perimeter of the buildings. A soft red light lit up the outside of both buildings. The light was easy on his eyes and helped him see the surrounding area without blinding him.

There was a glow of white lights inside both buildings as well. He observed the building that looked more like a living space. There were curtains over the windows, so he could not tell if there was any movement inside. The hour was still early. He suspected that whoever inhabited the dwelling would still be awake.

There was an old human transport out front. Even from this distance he could see there was damage to the front window and left front side. He silently padded across the open area to the transport. His cat sniffed the front corner. The faint smell of blood clung to the vehicle. His sharp eyes narrowed on a few strands of blue-black hair. He sneered when he realized that Walkyr d'Rojah must have collided with the transport in his hasty escape from the avalanche he had caused.

He decided to go into the large boxy building first and then the smaller dwelling. After all, Walkyr might be in this one. He circled around the building again until he reached a side entrance. He shape-shifted and scanned the area using his more effective feline senses before turning to his two-legged form. Pulling his laser pistol from the holster at his waist, he fired at the light before aiming at the door's locking mechanism. In seconds, he slipped through the door and into the building.

~

Trescina rounded the last curve in the road leading to rescue center. She slowed when she saw another car approaching. Turning on her signal, she was surprised when the other car did the same.

She pulled into the driveway and braked harder then she should have. The Suburban slid several feet before stopping. She looked in the mirror and recognized Heather's SUV pulling in behind her.

"Wait here," she said, running her hand over Cinnamon's head when the tigress stuck it between the seats.

She undid her seatbelt and opened the door. Heather pulled up behind her and powered down the window. Trescina breathed a sigh of relief when she saw that Zeke was sitting in the passenger seat.

"Hi, Trescina, is everything okay? Did the cat take a turn for the worse?" Heather anxiously asked.

Trescina shook her head. "No, he's alright. Listen, I know this is going to sound strange, but I… don't think it is safe for you to go home at the moment," she said.

Heather looked at her with a startled expression. "Why not?" she replied.

Zeke lowered the cell phone in his hand and leaned forward to look at her. "Is it because of the aliens that were shooting at each other?" Zeke asked.

Heather turned her head to glare at her son. "Zeke," Heather started to reprimand.

"Yes," Trescina replied.

"Told you I was telling the truth," Zeke muttered, returning to the game he was playing.

Trescina almost winced when Heather turned her head and looked at her with a disbelieving expression. She looked at the woman with an apologetic smile. The cat was out of the bag now.

"I'm having enough trouble with Zeke without you helping him make up stuff, Trescina," Heather retorted, rather exasperated.

Trescina touched Heather's arm. "He's not making it up, Heather. The leopard this morning is not what you think. He's... he's an alien shape-shifter from another planet," she quietly explained.

Heather shook her head and shot her a wounded expression. "I can't believe that you would lie to me. How am I supposed to teach him right from wrong if he thinks he can say things like this?" she said.

"I'm not lying," Zeke muttered under his breath, not looking up from his game.

"He's not lying, Heather," Trescina confirmed.

Heather turned her head and stared out of the windshield. Trescina felt a sense of desperation when the other woman's hand dropped to the gearshift. She knew that Heather was going to ignore her.

"I can prove it," she suddenly blurted out.

Heather paused and shot Trescina a heated glare. Trescina could feel her cat's protest, but she didn't know what else to do. She could only hope that Heather would accept what she was about to see and realize that no one would believe her if she said anything.

"How? Are you going to ask the alien cat that Terry hit to suddenly turn into a little green man?" Heather sarcastically demanded.

Zeke snorted. "He's not little, and he definitely wasn't green," he snickered, turning his cell phone off so he could look curiously at Trescina. "Is one of your tigers a shape-shifting alien?" he asked.

Trescina shook her head. "No.... I am," she replied.

She gave Zeke a wry smile when she saw his eyes widen before turning her own eyes back to Heather's face. Reaching in, she touched Heather's arm and waited for the other woman to look at her. The shimmer of tears and the deep hurt she saw reflected in the woman's eyes surprised her.

"Please... I need you to understand and... well, to not tell anyone about what you see," she pleaded.

"What is there to tell?" Heather asked in a bitter tone.

"This," she replied before she stepped back from the SUV.

Trescina could feel her cat's resignation. A second later, she was peering in the window of Heather's SUV with a feline's worried expression. Heather's mouth hung open, and her face turned extremely pale. She looked over from Heather to Zeke when the boy sprawled over his mom to look out the window at her.

"That is totally awesome!" he breathed.

His voice appeared to trigger a reaction in Heather. She was frantically trying to push her son back into his seat. It wasn't difficult to sense that the other woman was about to bolt. She shape-shifted back into her two-legged form and reached out to grab the window before Heather could roll her window up again.

"Heather, please listen to me. One minute, just give me one minute. Please," she pleaded.

"I...," Heather choked out, leaning away from her.

Trescina saw Heather look at Zeke when he touched his mom's arm. "Please, Mom. The other guy—he saved my life. Listen to what Ms. Trescina has to say," he encouraged.

Heather drew in a shaky breath and looked at Zeke with a suddenly fierce expression. "You are going to be grounded for life," she declared in her fiercest angry mom voice.

Zeke chuckled and sat back in his seat. "That's like my millionth life.

You'll never get grandkids if you don't let me out of the house," he teased.

Heather groaned and slumped in her seat. Trescina gave Zeke a wink when the boy grinned at her and gave her the thumbs up. She could also see the excitement in his eyes, and thankfully his cell phone was on the floorboard. She hoped he didn't realize he'd just missed the chance to go viral. Her lips twitched when he suddenly bent and picked up the cell phone with a groan and shot her a hopeful look.

"This is top secret," she sternly ordered.

Heather reached out and plucked Zeke's phone out of his hand. "Payback, Zeke, remember that. Mothers never forget," she muttered before turning her attention to Trescina. "You have one minute."

Trescina nodded and drew in a deep breath. "I never knew I was an alien until I met Walkyr this morning, and he told me that he was an alien from a planet called Sarafin. There are some bad guys that came here looking for something, but I'm not sure what it is. I think my mom and I came from this Sarafin planet, too, but I don't want anyone to know because I'm still trying to figure out everything.

"My mom was murdered by poachers when I was a child and she never told my dad—only he really wasn't my dad; he was my stepdad. My sister and I are pretty sure the man who killed our mom murdered him. My sister isn't an alien—well, she is but only half, and she can't do the things I can. You are the first person I've ever told this to, and I think one of the bad guys followed the trail Zeke left yesterday, and he may be at your house. I need you to keep all of this a secret," Trescina finished breathlessly.

She looked at Heather and waited—and waited—and waited. The woman was staring at her as if she had two heads instead of simply having the ability to shape-shift into a cat. Trescina bit her lip when the silence stretched out longer than she was given to explain.

"Both of your parents were murdered?" Heather whispered, her eyes filling with tears.

"Yes," Trescina replied with a slight nod.

"Oh my God. I couldn't even imagine… and then not knowing where you came from," Heather murmured.

"Mom, she's an alien! How cool is that?" Zeke said.

Heather turned and glared at her son again. "And you almost got yourself killed by one, young man. Now will you listen when I tell you that taking off without telling anyone can be dangerous?" she scolded.

Zeke grinned. "Yeah, you were right," he replied.

Heather groaned again and leaned her head back against the headrest. Trescina felt a shaft of sympathy for Heather. If Zeke was this bad now, she couldn't imagine what he would be like in another year or two.

"I'll deal with you later, smart butt." Heather reprimanded her son and then looked at her. "What do you want me to do?"

Trescina squeezed Heather's arm in support. "Until I can scout out whether it is safe or not, you might want to stay somewhere else. You could go to my house. It should be safe, but… well, with Walkyr there, it might not be if the men come looking for him there," she murmured.

Heather shook her head. "We can go to the ranch. I stay in the apartment above the barn at least once a week to check the animals there. Oh, God, I forgot that I'm supposed to have the high school kids come out here tomorrow," she suddenly groaned.

"Why don't you have them go to the ranch instead," Zeke suggested.

Heather nodded. "That's a good idea," she said.

Zeke shrugged. "I have them on occasion. Can I have my phone back?" he asked, already bored with the conversation.

Trescina chuckled when Heather rolled her eyes. Her expression sobered when Heather looked at her again. She could see the uneasiness in the woman's eyes even though Heather was trying to hide it.

"I need to think about what I've learned. I… can't promise I won't report this. I won't say anything until I can wrap my own head around everything," Heather quietly said.

Trescina's gut tightened. Before, she had kept the secret of her existence because she was afraid of what would happen to her and her sister. Now, it was obvious that there were greater influences involved—powers from another world.

"Think of what it would do to the planet, Heather. People aren't ready to know there is other life out there. You need to think about what would happen to you… and to Zeke," Trescina cautioned.

"But… what if the… they plan to attack us, and I say nothing?" Heather whispered.

Trescina shook her head. "Walkyr said they don't want to alarm us. He just wants to find the men who came here and return to his own world," she reassured Heather as she stepped back from the SUV.

"No promises, but… I'll think about what you said," she replied, rolling up the window.

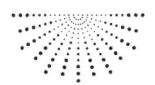

CHAPTER FIFTEEN

Miami, Florida

The unpleasant smell of cigarette smoke filled the air. The heavy-set man leaning against the side of the car lifted the butt of the almost finished cigarette to his mouth. He drew in one last breath before he dropped the remains to the ground and stepped on it.

Vladimir Mirvo, pulled a handkerchief from the front pocket of his black trousers and wiped his brow. An expression of irritation swept across his face. Why anyone would want to live in such a godforsaken place was beyond him. Here it was winter, and he was sweating his ass off.

He straightened when he heard the squealing of tires as a car turned into the otherwise empty parking lot of a building under construction. The car pulled up beside his.

"Vlad?" the man called above the rumble of the engine.

He gave a brief nod and watched as the man turned the engine off and climbed out of the bright yellow Corvette convertible. The man looked just like he sounded on the phone. The old man climbed out of the car with an agility that belied his age.

Vlad waited as Carl Roland rounded his car. He looked with distaste at the man when he held out his hand. After a few seconds, Carl dropped his hand to his side as if he'd never extended it.

Vlad studied the man he'd hired to find the location of the person he was hunting. Carl had a bushy mustache, weighed barely over a hundred and twenty pounds dripping wet, and had to be in his early seventies. A pair of dark, oversized aviator sunglasses hid the man's eyes. Dressed in a partially buttoned, tropical print shirt, white shorts, and tan deck shoes, Carl looked every bit the part of a classic bookie.

"You know, you look very much like some Russian mafia goon," Carl chuckled, his accent still laced with his New Jersey roots.

"Do you have the information I requested?" Vlad demanded, ignoring Carl's cheerful reflection.

Carl pulled his sunglasses down a little and looked over the top of the rim. "I think the more pertinent question is do you have the money?" the old man countered. He pushed his sunglasses back into place while he waited for Vlad's response.

Vlad turned, reached through the window of the rental car, and pulled an envelope off the dash. He handed the bulging white rectangle to Carl who quickly opened it and counted the one hundred dollar bills. The older man grinned, nodded, and dropped the envelope onto the passenger seat of his car before he picked up a large manila folder and held it out.

"You'll find everything you requested inside," Carl said.

Vlad silently pulled out the contents of the folder and thumbed through them. The assorted documents might look legitimate to an untrained eye, but Vlad knew they were phonies. However, there were several images of Trescina Bukov-Danshov included with the forged documents, as well as a location listed.

He slid the items back into the folder and tossed it through the window before opening the driver's door to his car and sliding into the seat. He started the car and glanced out of the window when Carl stepped back.

"It was nice doing business with you. If you need anything else, don't hesitate to contact me," Carl called.

Vlad punched the accelerator and drove away without answering. He reached into the console between the front seats, picked up his cell phone, and impatiently punched in a number.

"Location?" a woman's voice requested in Russian.

"Wyoming. I need a one-way ticket and a rental car," Vlad responded.

"When?" she asked.

"Today," he answered.

"Please give me a moment," she responded.

Vlad slowed as the cars ahead of him came to a stop at a traffic light. His attention moved back to the folder. One of the images of Trescina had slipped out when he threw the folder onto the seat. He picked it up and studied the face of the woman who had her arm wrapped around a snow leopard. Most people would think the darker marks on her face were caused by the bad picture quality. He knew differently. They were there because of who and *what* she was.

Someone honked a horn behind him, drawing his attention back to the road. The cars in front of him were beginning to move. He placed the picture on top of the folder and pressed the accelerator.

The car behind him sped up to get beside him. The young man who was driving started to give him the finger until Vlad turned his head to look at him. The man's eyes widened when he saw the scars on Vlad's cheek. A cruel smile curved Vlad's lips when the man accelerated and pulled away.

"This time, I have you," he murmured to himself.

"Sir, I can book a flight for you at four o'clock this afternoon. Is that time good for you?" the woman came back on the line.

"Yes, that will suit me just fine," he replied.

∽

Trescina bit her lip as Heather backed out onto the highway and drove away. She watched the taillights of the car disappear before she turned back to the Suburban. A soft smile curved her lips when Trescina saw that she had left the driver's door open. Cinnamon was patiently waiting for her, standing with her front paws in the driver's seat and her head out the door. She walked back to the vehicle and gave Cinnamon a huge hug.

"I'm not sure what to do," she groaned.

"I will tell you what you will do—you will never scare me the way you did when I realized what you were thinking," Walkyr's deep voice growled.

Trescina jumped and turned around. She lifted a hand to her pounding chest. Even her cat was taken by surprise, which seldom ever happened.

"Walkyr! You scared nine lives off of me," she chastised in a breathless tone.

She warily watched as he strode out of the woods toward her. Spice trotted by his side. Cinnamon pushed past her and jumped out of the SUV. Trescina frowned when she saw that Spice was breathing heavily.

"What happened to Spice?" she demanded.

Walkyr drew to a stop in front of her. He placed his hands on each side of her, effectively caging her between his body and the car. She swallowed when she saw twin flames of gold burning in his eyes.

Strange, I don't remember his eyes having that much gold in them, she silently thought.

"It was a long run from where you left us," he commented.

Trescina swallowed. She looked at Spice again, her concern that he'd seen her shape-shift dissipating at the sight of Spice's heaving sides. She looked back at Walkyr's riveting face.

"I was hoping you'd..." her voice died when he leaned down and pressed his lips to hers.

A soft moan escaped her, and she ran her hands up his chest. She gripped his shoulders and parted her lips. He opened his mouth when she tentatively ran her tongue along his top lip.

He moved his hands to her forearms and quickly took over the kiss. She took several deep breaths when he lifted his head.

"That shouldn't have happened," she said, looking at his chest.

He gently lifted her chin. "Yes, it should. My cat recognizes you as his mate. While I tried to deny it at first, I have to agree with him. This is another gift from the Goddess, our ability to recognize our mate the moment we meet," he ruefully informed her.

Trescina felt her cat's indignation at his words, and the knowledge of what had been happening clicked into place. Her cat's insistence that they run was not because she was afraid of Walkyr, she had recognized Walkyr as her mate, and she had been afraid of what that would mean.

I not admitting, her cat pouted.

You rotten little...! Argh! Now I understand how Heather feels when she's dealing with Zeke, Trescina retorted.

"Trescina.... Trescina, you need not be afraid. I will not do anything to harm you... or frighten you. I have learned a thing or two from my brothers' interactions with their mates," he reassured her.

"This is not the time or the place," she said with a shake of her head and looked away from him. "I don't know for sure, but I think one of the guys you are looking for may have followed the tracks left by Zeke."

∼

Walkyr looked down the dark road that led to the two buildings he had noticed through the trees. He and Spice had already picked up on the other Sarafin's tracks as well as scented the traitor's path to the building that housed the animals, but he had steered clear of the building when he saw the faint shimmer of light through the trees and noticed that Trescina's transport was not out front.

He had breathed a sigh of relief when he saw her standing at the driver's door hugging Cinnamon. He had replayed everything that happened since he first saw Trescina as he ran through the woods. It was hard to believe that his first day with her hadn't ended yet.

He remembered the first time he saw her standing in the doorway looking at him with a combination of fear and determination.

Holding knife, his cat reminded him.

Holding a knife in her hand, he chuckled.

He remembered the soft brush of her breath tickling his ear as she threatened to kill him. *Was that only this morning?* he thought in disbelief. He couldn't believe that so much had happened in one day.

Perhaps days longer here, his cat suggested.

He frowned and looked at Trescina. She was looking at him with an expectant expression. It took him a moment to realize that he was still holding her. He released her and stepped back.

"How many hours are in this planet's day?" he asked curiously.

She blinked at him in confusion. "Twenty-four. Why?" she asked.

He shrugged. "I feel like I have known you much longer," he said before turning his attention back to the long driveway. "I will take care of the other traitor. This time, stay here and lock yourself in your transport." His stern voice surprised her a bit.

Trescina raised an eyebrow at his tone. "I'm not helpless, and I'm not too stupid to live. I won't stay in the Suburban like a good little girl. Take the tigers with you. I'll find a secure place and keep a look-out in case anyone else comes," she said.

Walkyr frowned at her. "The other man died during the avalanche. I found his ashes mixed in with the snow near their ship," he said.

"That's fine, but I seem to remember there are two more that you still haven't located," she reminded him.

He gave her a sharp-toothed grin. "I haven't forgotten. I found no other tracks, but I have a plan to draw them out," he said with a mysterious smirk. "Stay hidden. If I am distracted by worrying about you, I could make a mistake."

She pursed her lips before she reluctantly nodded. Walkyr loved the look of heated protest in her eyes. Excitement built in him when he thought of the future. If this was what his brothers felt, he could understand why they loved waking every day in their mate's arms and acted like wet cats when they were torn away.

"I'll be back," he promised, leaning forward to brush a kiss against her lips. She softly chuckled at his words. "What is it?"

"I have an alien telling me that *'I'll be back'*," she replied with a shake of her head. "You wouldn't understand."

A puzzled expression crossed his features before he turned away from her. He motioned for the two tigers to follow him. He considered several different scenarios on how the tigers could distract the traitor that had survived the avalanche—without putting either of them in danger. He was surprised when a different image appeared in his head —an image of a sleek black tiger with beautiful blue-black stripes that matched the spots on his own coat.

As quickly as the image appeared, it vanished. If he'd had more time, he would have tried to learn where the Siberian tigers had seen such an unusual tiger before. His cat purred, confusing him even more.

Shape-shift, he commanded, pushing away the distracting thoughts that could get them killed.

Only one dying is traitor, his cat vowed with deadly intent as one by one, he and the two tigers slipped through the open side door.

CHAPTER SIXTEEN

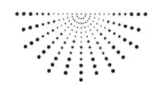

*T*rescina paced back and forth along the road. She was uncertain about what to do. Should she run or stay? She knew nothing about the mating of her species. Obviously her cat knew just enough to keep her in the dark.

Thanks a lot for that! I swear this has to be the longest day of my life, she silently groaned.

She had just turned around when she saw the headlights of an approaching truck. An expletive that would have gotten her mouth washed out with soap as a child flashed through her mind when she saw the truck slowing down. Surprise filled her when the lights suddenly went out as the truck skidded to a stop a short distance from the Suburban.

"What?! Mason.... Chad.... What are you two...?" her voice faded when she saw them exit the truck carrying hunting rifles. She lifted her hands and started toward them as a sense of fear engulfed her. "What are you doing?"

"Are you alright, Trescina?" Chad demanded, his gaze sweeping the area.

"Yes...," once again her voice faded, and she silently groaned.

Heather must have told the men. The way they were looking around spoke volumes. She was about to make up a story when the back doors of the truck opened and two other men stepped out. The weapons in their hands were different—so was the way they were dressed.

She warily watched as the four men walked closer to her. The last two men who had exited the truck took up a position on each side of her. Her hand went to her stomach when her cat hissed and clawed at her as they leaned closer and sniffed her. Out of instinct, she shoved the one closest to her and hissed.

"*Cat's balls,* what is a Sarafin female doing here?" the man that she had shoved exclaimed.

"She smells like Walkyr," the other man stated.

She hurried toward Mason and Chad. "Who are these clowns?" she demanded.

Mason grimaced and nodded. "The one you shoved is Qadir. The other one is Pallu. I think I got that right," he introduced.

"Where is Walkyr?" Qadir questioned.

The one named Pallu grinned. "I'd like to know why she smells like him," he said.

"I smell like him because I was holding a knife to his throat this morning," she snapped. "Who are you?"

Chad walked over to her and placed his hand on her arm. "They are Walkyr's brothers. At least that is what they say," he added with an uneasy look toward the two men.

Her eyes narrowed with suspicion. "Walkyr said there were two other men from the traitors' ship," she countered.

"And when did he tell you that? Before or after you held a knife to his throat? Or was it when you were draped over him?" Qadir sarcastically asked.

"F... you," Trescina growled.

Pallu's eyes lit up. "I know what that means. Pearl says it means...," he started to say.

"I know what it means too," Qadir snapped. "I want to know where Walkyr is."

Trescina swallowed. She had heard Walkyr mention Pearl's name. The bad guys wouldn't know who she was, or if they did, they wouldn't mention her with humor the way Pallu did. The more she studied the two men, the more she could see a family resemblance to Walkyr in their eyes, nose, mouth, and chin.

"He went to the rescue center. We found tracks leading from a spaceship that Walkyr said belonged to the traitors. Someone was following the tracks Zeke left behind. Walkyr said that it was one of the traitors. One man was already killed, and he didn't know where the other two had gone. He said he had a plan to draw them out," she quietly explained, pointing down the driveway before she wrapped her arms around her waist.

All four men looked in the direction she had pointed before silently looking at each other.

"Heather's house is behind the main building. There is an entrance in the front, one on the side, and a large receiving door in the back," Chad explained to the men.

"Stay here. It is best if we deal with this ourselves, if Walkyr hasn't taken care of the traitor already," Qadir ordered.

"Wait!" Trescina looked at the two men. "There... My tigers are with Walkyr. Don't hurt them. They are white Siberians—a male and a female. The male is named Spice and the female is Cinnamon," she pleaded.

Pallu smiled in understanding. "We'll send them back to you. Qadir and I can save Walkyr's butt. We've done it plenty of times before," he teased.

"Thank you," she said.

She watched as the two men shape-shifted and took off down the long winding driveway. Only when they had disappeared from sight did she turn to look at Chad and Mason who were still scanning the area with wary eyes, their rifles at the ready.

She tilted her head to the side and stared at Chad with an accusing expression. Chad grimaced, looked away from her, and remained silent. Mason saw her look and shrugged. He stepped closer to her before he quietly spoke.

"It's a long story, but Paul lives in outer space on a planet called Valdier with his wife, Morian, and his daughter, Trisha, and her family. The aliens like to use the ranch as their personal base on Earth. Of course, we don't advertise it for obvious reasons. We'd deeply appreciate it if you'd keep this information to yourself," Mason explained with an almost apologetic expression.

"What about Heather and Zeke?" Trescina quietly asked.

Mason sighed. "Ann Marie is trying to explain everything to her," he admitted.

"I have a question for you, Trescina," Chad said, turning to look at her with a piercing look.

Trescina's body stiffened. "Wh…what would you like to know?" she hesitantly asked.

Chad turned to study her face. "Why did Qadir refer to you as a Sarafin female?" he inquired.

Trescina trembled. Her fear that Heather or Zeke had revealed her secret evaporated. Her head was shaking in denial even before she choked out the words. "I don't know what you mean," she lied.

Chad's expression softened. "I think you do," he gently contradicted.

Walkyr slowly crept forward. The two tigers silently moved down the long hallway. They cautiously slipped through the opposing doors on each side that led into the exam rooms. Each section of exam rooms opened to another corridor. On the right side, it opened to a large room divided into a section for receiving and lab testing. On the left, Walkyr could see the spacious cages that were stacked from floor to ceiling along the wall.

He shape-shifted and pulled the laser pistol from the holster at his hip. He stepped into one of the rooms on the left. It looked as if this room was used for operating on the poor beasts that were sick or injured. He shuddered to think of such primitive methods of healing.

In the other room, he heard the screech of a terrified animal. He wasn't sure if it was one of the tigers until he heard a soft growl of warning from Spice. He'd found the traitor.

Walkyr.

Walkyr stiffened when he felt the familiar mental touch of his brother, Qadir, reaching out to him. He glanced over his shoulder with a frown. Their connection in this form only worked if they were in close proximity. He saw Spice pause in the doorway across from him. The tiger stared at him as if waiting for guidance. Walkyr sent an image of his brother in both his two-legged and leopard form with a sense of calm to let the tiger know not to attack.

Where are you? Walkyr replied.

Pallu and I are coming in now. Is the traitor here? Qadir replied.

Yes, down the corridor and to the left. He is moving through the animal holding area. I am in the third room on the left, he answered.

Send the tigers out. We will take care of this, Qadir instructed.

Walkyr sent a silent command to Trescina's tigers to return and protect their mistress. He watched as Spice exited the room across from his and silently moved toward the open door. He peered around the corner to make sure that Cinnamon had also followed his instructions.

He saw the tigress following the male at the same time as he caught sight of the shadowy forms of his brothers.

Pallu had shape-shifted into his two-legged form while Qadir still retained his cat form. This would allow Qadir to connect the three of them and they could work as one. He motioned for Pallu to go up through the right corridor while he and Qadir approached from the left. Pallu nodded and disappeared.

Is there just this one? Qadir asked.

Yes. I think he is looking for me, Walkyr stated as an idea formed.

What are you going to do? Pallu questioned with a slightly resigned tone.

We need him alive to give us information. He is searching for me. There is a holding room at the far corner of the building. Pallu work your way around. I hope you have one of those poison strips on you. We may need it. Qadir, be ready to attack. I think it is time I played dead, Walkyr chuckled.

Walkyr returned his pistol to his holster as a new plan formed. They needed information. Killing the traitor wouldn't help them learn how far the treachery had gone. He shimmered as he shape-shifted. He silently crossed the corridor and moved down the hall to the room where he had woken after his accident.

He slipped through the open door, nudged it closed behind him, and took up a position on the thick padding. The soft tread of footsteps told him that he had barely made it into the room in time. His cat bristled at playing dead. He wanted to attack.

Walkyr calmed his cat. If this traitor used the same tactics the others had, the man would be dead from poison before Walkyr could restrain him. With his brothers' help, they could use the element of surprise to capture him and force the antidote strip into the warrior's mouth. They would have seconds—depending on the warrior's determination to commit suicide.

The sound of the door opening was his cue to look up with a dazed expression. Ranker's face lit up with triumphant satisfaction as he aimed his laser pistol at Walkyr.

"You have no idea how long I've wanted to do this," Ranker stated.

"Not as long nor as much as we have, I'm sure," Qadir replied from behind the man.

Walkyr rolled to the side and jumped to his feet at the same time as Ranker's finger depressed the trigger on the laser pistol. The blast cut a scorching path across the pad, setting it on fire. Walkyr assumed his human form in the blink of an eye and grabbed for Ranker's outstretched arm at the same time as Qadir pulled the man backwards and off balance.

Ranker's furious roar sent the animals in the back of the rescue center into a panic. Their loud calls of terror added to the chaos. Walkyr ripped the pistol from Ranker's hand and held him down while Pallu kneeled on the man's other arm. Ranker bent his head and bit down on a section of his vest. Foam began to bubble from between his lips.

"Open your mouth," Pallu growled.

Ranker defiantly glared up at them. Walkyr could see the glaze of death starting to settle over the man's eyes. A malicious smile curved his lips.

"Keep your mouth closed through this," he snarled, bringing his knee up into Ranker's groin.

"Got it," Pallu stated as he shoved the strip between Ranker's lips when the man's eyes widened and his lips parted on an agonized groan from the intense pain.

Qadir looked over at Walkyr and grinned. *"Cat's balls,* but that was low. Does your mate know you fight dirty?" he chuckled.

"How do you know my mate?" Walkyr demanded.

He released his hold on Ranker when the man suddenly went limp after Pallu placed a sedative patch on his neck. Pushing up off the ground, he glared at his brother. Qadir paused in the process of flipping Ranker over onto his stomach so he could restrain the man's wrists behind his back.

"She is at the end of the driveway with the two humans Vox told us to contact. What were you thinking? I can't believe you brought your mate on a mission with you," Qadir said in a tone filled with disapproval.

"I never knew you had a mate, Walkyr. You didn't mention it back on our world," Pallu added. "I don't even know how you got her onto the long distance transport. Gable never said anything either."

Walkyr looked back and forth between his brothers. They were both giving him dirty looks. He shook his head.

"I don't know what you are talking about. I just met Trescina this morning—or yesterday morning depending on the time here," he said, pulling their very groggy prisoner to his feet for transporting.

"This morning! That's impossible," Pallu exclaimed, looking at Qadir in confusion.

Walkyr frowned. "Why is it impossible? You know that our cats recognize our mates immediately, often before we do. What's so surprising that I found my mate here on Earth? Vox and Viper are both mated to human females," he replied with a shrug.

Qadir looked at him with a mixture of disbelief and amusement. "You don't know, do you?" he prodded.

Walkyr's frown deepened. "Know what?" he demanded.

Pallu grinned. "That Trescina isn't a human. She's definitely a Sarafin female," he said, reaching out to grab Ranker when Walkyr suddenly let go of the man.

"Sarafin.... How....?" he started to protest when the image the two tigers had sent him earlier formed in his mind again. "Black tiger with blue stripes.... She has stripes. She covers them.... *Cat's Balls*!" he snarled, thrusting past Qadir and striding down the corridor.

"And I always thought he was the observant one," Pallu commented behind him.

"You'd better go after him. I'll take this one up to the ship," Qadir said with a shake of his head. "Mates! Who needs them?! Who wants them?!"

CHAPTER SEVENTEEN

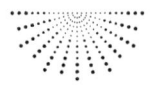

Trescina raced through the house gathering as many items as she could. She shoved the clothes out of her dresser drawer into one bag and the few pictures she had of her family into another. She would have to leave some things behind.

At this point, she didn't care anymore. She could always replace most of the material things if she needed to do so. She was more concerned with the few sentimental items that she had left from her mother and stepfather.

She was too stressed to cry. Instead, she channeled that emotion into action. Spice looked at her with mild curiosity while Cinnamon followed her from room to room, a quiet, supportive shadow.

"It's okay, sweetheart, I won't leave you or your brother behind," she promised, running a loving hand over the tigress' head.

Trescina lifted a hand and pushed her hair out of her eyes. With a frustrated growl, she went into the bathroom, opened a drawer, and pulled out a hairband. She grabbed her hair and twisted it up and off her face before she wound the elastic hair tie around the mass to keep it out of her way.

She looked in the mirror and froze. Her eyes looked too big for her face at the moment. The makeup that she normally wore to cover the markings had disappeared. Now the tiger stripes that ran from her temple down her right cheek and neck before spreading across her shoulders and chest were plainly visible. She shook her head and refocused on what she needed to do.

The moment the tigers had reappeared, she piled them into the Suburban and took off. Walkyr didn't need her help any longer. He had his two brothers, as well as Mason and Chad. They should be more than enough to take on one measly alien traitor.

She gazed at the tigers while she zipped up one of the bags. At first she hadn't been sure what she would do and where she should go. Then it had dawned on her—why not join Katarina and the circus? The members of the circus were always on the move and very protective of her sister and her pets. She would also blend in better with the circus members and there wouldn't be any aliens to worry about!

Satisfied with her plans, she grabbed one of the bags and carried it out to the Suburban that she had parked in the garage. She would call her sister once she was on the road. Her first stop would be to South Florida where she would pick up her truck and camper. Then she would find out where Katarina was and meet up with her. It was the perfect plan, she concluded.

Except mate, her cat snipped.

"Oh no you don't. You were the one who kept yelling 'run' if I remember correctly. Don't start whining now about mates. I'm not...," her voice faded when her throat tightened. "What am I supposed to do with an alien?"

It was impossible. No, run, keep going, and don't look back. She'd lived her life like that ever since Vladimir Mirvo returned to kidnap her and her sister, Katarina. Killing their mother hadn't been enough for the poacher. He wanted to capture them and sell them to the highest bidder.

There were a lot of sick people in the world and Vladimir Mirvo was one of the worst of them. He justified everything he did by how much money he could make—even murder. She and Katarina knew he was responsible for their father's death, but Mirvo knew a lot of politicians, judges, and members of law enforcement that owed favors to different people.

She had enough issues without adding alien shape-shifting warriors and far-off worlds to her list. If that wasn't enough to convince her to run, the idea of living on another planet was enough to send her screaming. No, sometimes it was good to know your limitations and this was hers.

She returned to the house and looked around the room. She had rented the house furnished, and she had not added much since her arrival. There was only one more thing that she needed to retrieve—the necklace that her mother had given her.

"Ok, I'll get the necklace, and we can be on the road. If you two need to go to the bathroom, you'd better do it now," she warned the two tigers.

Spice yawned while Cinnamon turned and headed for the door leading out to the garage. She scowled at the male tiger. He was notorious for wanting to stop and mark the mile marker post every ten miles.

"You'd better go, Spice. I'm not stopping this time," she threatened.

The tiger snorted when she sent him a mental impression of him having to hold his bladder. He rose to his feet and quickly disappeared down the hallway. Her surprised chuckle of amusement echoed through the room. They really were such amusing characters.

"That will teach him," she muttered, returning to her bedroom to gather the last, most important gift from her childhood, the necklace that her mother called *The* Heart of the Cat.

∽

"No response," Airabus quietly shared.

Raul's face tightened. The fingers of his metal hand curled into a fist strong enough to crush rock. He looked at the holographic map of the region hovering above the makeshift table they were using.

"We will return to the ship," he replied.

Airabus' expression remained neutral. "What about *The* Heart of the Cat?" he asked.

Raul looked at the map again. "The last signal was six months ago. It was tracked to this area before the signal stopped. We've detected nothing since then," he said.

Airabus sat back against the wall of their portable shelter. This was the end of the first week of their search, and they had discovered nothing but endless snowy terrain and a wide variety of beasts in different sizes. They intentionally avoided the few human dwellings that were scattered among the mountains and forests.

"We could return to the ship, move it to a different location, and continue monitoring. Are you sure that the signal is the one mentioned in the scrolls?" Airabus pressed.

Raul snarled and swept his hand across the table, sending his cup, the holographic mapping device, and the glove he normally wore over his metal hand and arm to the ground. Airabus silently rose and retrieved the items. He was about to store the holographic map when it emitted a distinctive chime. His hand froze in midair, and he looked up at Airabus.

The other man turned and looked at the map. Raul had told him that the holographic mapping device was known as the key. Centuries ago, Raul had stolen it out of the ancient archives. He had returned again for the scroll that would describe *The* Heart of the Cat and tell him how to harness the power of the Goddess, but it was taken before he could safely retrieve it without being caught.

Realizing that he might be suspected in the disappearance, he had returned home to serve the King and Queen as their Captain of the

Guard. He had requested Airabus join him. Not long after his return, Raul had set his sights on the young Princess.

Each step had been carefully planned and plotted. Raul's goal was to learn the royal secrets, be accepted into the Royal family and gain the trust of Queen Mia in the hopes of discovering everything he could about *The* Heart of the Cat. Raul eventually learned of Queen Mia's abduction from the royal family when he uncovered the sealed documents hidden beneath the palace. He had discovered that the first Queen Mia was actually the direct descendant of one of the original four brothers who'd been given the gift of *The* Heart of the Cat.

The first Queen Mia had been unable to carry a cub. In desperation, she had sought the help of a surrogate to carry the King and Queen's child. The Queen had died before the child was born. Devastated by the death of his mate, the King soon followed her in death.

Eventually, one of the healers revealed what the King and Queen had done. The council decided to bring their young Queen home; and so, when she was little more than a cub, the new Queen Mia was stolen from her surrogate family and returned to her rightful home. She would later give birth to another girl, Princess Mia Elena, who would fall in love with the handsome Captain of the Guard, Raul T'Rivre.

Airabus shook his head and stared down at the holographic map. He placed it on the table. Raul stepped closer, his dark eyes glittering with determination and greed. The silence grew to a deafening roar before another chime filled the small area.

"We've found it," Raul murmured, looking at him with hard, glittering eyes. "Mark the location. We need to leave immediately."

～

Raul couldn't believe that they had been less than a mile from *The* Heart of the Cat. It had only taken a few minutes to pack up their camp. If he had known that the gem he spent centuries searching for was so close, he would have left everything behind.

The signal led them to a small yellow and white frame house. They watched from the shadows as a human female carried things out to a transport.

The signal was strong here. *The* Heart of the Cat must have been deposited here centuries ago where it remained undetected until recently. His eyes narrowed on the slender young woman. She had dark hair that she had piled onto the top of her head. There was something about her that felt vaguely familiar to him. Perhaps it was the graceful way she moved. It had been a long time since he'd noticed how a woman moved.

"What do you wish to do?" Airabus quietly asked.

Raul glanced at Airabus. At one time he would have considered the man a friend, but his need for friendship had died centuries ago. Now all he needed in his life were those who could fulfill his commands.

"Return to the ship and make sure that Ranker and Nastran have repaired it. We need to depart as soon as I have the gem," Raul instructed.

"Don't you want me to help you retrieve *The* Heart of the Cat? I am here…," Airabus started to protest.

Raul lifted his metal hand. "I can handle a single human girl. It is imperative that we leave this planet before we cross paths with Walkyr d'Rojah," he impatiently replied.

Airabus reluctantly bowed his head in submission. "Yes, High Lord," he stiffly replied.

Raul waited until he knew Airabus had departed. He looked down at the key in his hand. The soft pulsing glow had turned to a bright, constant light. He looked up and slid the key into his pocket.

The human was coming out with a small case. She placed it in the front compartment of the vehicle and slammed the door. By the time she turned around, Raul was standing less than three feet from her.

She uttered a sharp, tense scream before clamping her lips together.

Her eyes were wide as she stared back at him, trying to see his features. A sardonic smile curved his lips. It wouldn't matter if she saw his features. She would soon be dead.

"Who the hell are you?" she blurted out.

Raul reached for his hood. He paused when her eyes locked on his metal arm, then slowly pushed back the hood of his cloak.

"You appear to have something I have been looking for, for a very long time," he stated.

Her chin lifted in surprising defiance. "I know you," she whispered.

He swept his gaze over her face, pausing on the marks along her temple. He took a step forward. He lifted his metal arm and wrapped his cold, hard fingers around her neck. She choked and wrapped her hands around his arm.

He ignored her struggle. Instead, he reached up and pulled off the band holding her hair. Long, dark curls cascaded down over her shoulders and fell across his arm. He continued to stare at her with cold, hard eyes.

"Well, well, well. It would appear I have finally found where my beloved mate took our daughter. Where is your mother?" he asked in a harsh voice.

CHAPTER EIGHTEEN

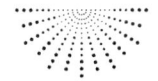

Walkyr gritted his teeth in irritation. He and Pallu rode in the back seat of the human's transport. He wanted to bang his head against the headrest of the front seat.

Pallu shot him a sympathetic look. "Their modes of transportation are very slow," he said.

"I could run faster than this," Walkyr growled under his breath.

"You two do know that we can hear everything you are saying even if we can't understand some of it, right?" Mason dryly commented, looking at the two of them in the rearview mirror.

Walkyr shot the older man a heated look of frustration. Due to the worsening weather conditions, Mason was now driving even more slowly than he had been before. It was barely snowing outside compared to many of the places he had travelled to in the past.

He took a deep, calming breath and turned to stare out of the window. He had to remind himself that if Mason felt it was necessary to drive this slowly, then maybe Trescina would have decided not to drive in it at all. He rubbed his hands together.

"What's wrong?" Pallu asked.

Walkyr looked at his younger brother before staring at his hands. He was as nervous as a kitten on his first day of school. A soft, unexpected chuckle escaped him, and he looked at his brother with amusement.

"I can't believe I didn't realize that she was one of us. I wonder how she came to be on Earth. When I first explained that I was an alien, she refused to believe me. It was like she had never even heard of an alien, much less seen one before," he shared.

"She wouldn't have if she was born and raised here," Chad reflected.

"But… How is that possible?" Pallu argued.

Chad turned in his seat. "Well, think about it. You guys have space travel. Haven't any of your kind been born on another world before?" he asked.

Walkyr thought about what Chad was saying but it still didn't make sense. Yes, they had been traveling to different worlds for centuries, but never this far before until a few years ago. This was an outlying planet. Still, it was possible. He would have to ask Trescina who her parents were and how they had come to be on this world.

"We're… Whoa! What the hell?" Mason suddenly exclaimed as he slammed on the brakes.

Cinnamon had her paws up on his window, and was making a series of coughing noises. He and Pallu reached for the handles of their doors at the same time. Scattered images flashed through his mind as he connected with the agitated tigress.

One strong emotion rose clearly and concisely in his mind—danger. Trescina was in grave danger. A savage snarl slipped from Walkyr. Cinnamon backed up and began pacing.

"What's going on?" Chad demanded, turning in his seat.

Walkyr looked across at the man. "Trescina is in danger. The man with the metal arm is here," he stated in a harsh voice.

"Man with a metal arm? Tell us what you want us to do," Chad replied in a grim tone.

"It is best if we handle it from here," Walkyr quietly stated.

Chad nodded in frustration. "We'll wait here," he replied.

Walkyr nodded and closed the door. He shifted into his cat and took off down the driveway at great speed. Behind him, he knew Pallu and Cinnamon were following him. He turned when he neared the house and disappeared into the trees that lined the side of the property.

The doors to her transport are open. It looks like she was planning to leave, Pallu noted.

Spice is in the cage, Walkyr noted, spying the male tiger agitatedly pacing back and forth in the confined space.

Does she cage her cats? Pallu asked with a slight sound of disdain in his voice before it cleared. *You?! Really? She had you locked in it? I would have loved to see that!*

Walkyr ignored his brother's amusement. Cinnamon must have shared that delightful little vision with Pallu. He would have to have a cat-to-cat talk with the two tigers when this was over. Spice paused his pacing and looked in their direction. He swiftly sent a soothing image to the tiger to remain calm and not make a sound.

Walkyr watched as the white tiger lowered himself down onto the pad and turned to stare at the door leading into the house. They didn't have many options available. The house had three entrances that he knew of. The one in the front, the one through the garage, and the large sliding glass doors in the back. Those would be difficult to break through because they were double paned glass if he remembered correctly.

What about a window? Pallu asked.

I haven't been through the back of the house. Stay here. I will check, Walkyr instructed.

Walkyr carefully worked his way around the perimeter of the house. He darted across the driveway and stealthily made his way to the opposite end of the house. He scanned the structure, searching for any possibility to enter without being heard. His cat's keen eyes noted that the small window was slightly ajar.

I'm going in.

I am, too, Pallu replied.

How? Walkyr demanded.

There are advantages to being the smallest brother, Pallu informed him with satisfaction.

An image of the large, square hatch in the door leading into the laundry room flashed through his mind. It would have been a very tight fit for him with the broader shoulders of his cat. Pallu's leopard was slightly smaller and definitely more agile. He and his other brothers used to fight over having Pallu on their team because his little brother could always get into places they couldn't.

He darted over to the window, keeping to the shadows. It would be light soon. He shape-shifted back to human form and pressed his back against the house. There was a soft glow of a light in the bathroom. He turned and peered through the gap in the window.

Looking at the window, he ran his hands along the screen protecting it. He bent and pulled a blade from his boot. He carefully worked the tip between the screen and the window frame. A few seconds later, he silently lifted the screen off and leaned it up against the house.

The window appeared to be relatively new and slid up without any noisy protest. Once it was opened as far as it would go, Walkyr shape-shifted again. It would be safer and easier to go through the window in his cat form.

I quiet, his cat gloated.

Just get us inside—without getting caught, he tersely ordered.

He felt the muscles of his cat tense before he easily sprang up, catching the sill with his front paws before pushing through the opening to land silently on the rug in front of the bathing unit. He immediately shape-shifted again so he could close the window to prevent any more heat from being lost. The last thing he wanted was a frigid draft of air to announce his arrival. Once he had closed the window, he moved to the closed door.

I'm in, he sent to his brother.

∼

Vlad set a long case on the ground and knelt beside it. He shrugged the white backpack off his shoulders and set it down on the snow next to him. The white thermal suit he was wearing kept him protected from the sub-zero temperatures.

He unzipped the backpack and pulled out a pair of military-grade thermal binoculars. His buyers had spared no expense on the equipment he required for this job. He looked forward to collecting on this one and on the next one for her sister.

Adjusting the focus, he peered through the lenses. He was two hundred yards from the house, but it seemed like he was just two feet away. The house had several lights on, making the night vision option unnecessary. He moved his head and braced his elbows on the firmly packed snow so that he could keep his arms steady as he surveilled the house. He carefully studied the silhouette of a person sitting in a chair by the large sliding glass doors. He returned his field of vision back to the seated person. The telltale dark curly hair was all he needed to identify his intended target. She was where the information he'd purchased said she would be.

"Finally, my little prize tigress. I have finally caught up with you," Vlad murmured.

Sitting back, he unzipped the long case, revealing the large rifle inside.

He quickly assembled the rifle before pulling out the portable tripod. He lay on his stomach and looked through the scope.

He had only been there for a few minutes when he realized that something was happening inside the house. He followed the movements of a man near his target. He released a series of sharp expletives when he saw the man toss away a tiger who had been with the woman just a moment ago. His finger remained frozen on the trigger until he saw the man reach for a weapon.

Vlad squeezed the trigger. The woman was of no use to him if she was dead. He moved the scope to search for the woman. He froze when he saw not one, but two men for a brief moment. He didn't recognize either of them, but they moved with power and grace. He didn't like so many new players suddenly showing up in his game. He didn't like it at all.

Pulling back, he silently packed up his equipment. It was better to retreat and attack another day than to end up like the man he had just killed. He had learned that lesson the day he received the scars that marred his face.

CHAPTER NINETEEN

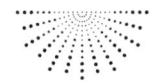

Minutes Ago:

Trescina rubbed her bruised throat and glared at the man standing in the shadows. She clenched her fist. The faint memories that had always been encased in a fog suddenly came into sharp focus.

She knew the memories were from her cat. Her primitive form retained the recessive memories of her connection with her mother while she was in the womb. Trescina remembered the gentle warmth of her mother's love even as pain and grief tore through her.

"She loved you," she forced out.

The man who was her biological father stared at her with indifference. Her gaze moved to his prosthetic arm before she looked away again. She had to get away from him and somehow alert Walkyr and his brothers.

"She was easily fooled and seduced," he coldly replied.

Trescina's lip curled. "You are a sick, twisted man. You had everything but you threw it away—for what? A metal arm and a miserably pathetic life," she sneered.

She didn't flinch when he took a step forward. He wouldn't get what he wanted. She would never let him have the gem that meant more to him than she and her mother ever had. If the story that Walkyr told her was true, the very existence of their species depended on her keeping it safe.

"Where is *The* Heart of the Cat?" he demanded.

"Where the sun doesn't shine. Why don't you stick your head up your ass and see if you can find it?" she sarcastically retorted.

She sat back in her chair when he took another step forward and raised his metal arm to strike her. Her cat snarled and clawed at her to let it loose. She was having difficulty controlling it.

Release me, her cat snarled.

"Do not think I will spare your life any more than I would have spared your mother's," he threatened, slowly lowering his arm.

Trescina brushed her hair away from her face, then released a cry of pain when he suddenly reached out and wrapped his cold, metal fingers around her forearm. She struggled to break free, clawing at his fingers.

"The mark…," he murmured, holding her arm at a painful angle to look at her wrist.

"It's… it's a tattoo… that I…," she lied.

Another cry of pain escaped her when he began to squeeze her arm tighter. Dots danced in front of her eyes, and she was sure that the bone in her arm was about to break. She gasped in relief when he suddenly released her.

"I don't need all of you, daughter. I am proof that a Sarafin warrior can survive without an arm, or his cat," he informed her with a cruel smile.

Shivers coursed through her when it dawned on her what he was saying. He could no longer shift. Either his cat refused to come forth or he refused to release it. In essence, he was a man who was already half dead.

She cradled her throbbing arm against her chest and stared at him in horror. His face was twisted into a savage mask of rage. Her heart ached for his cat imprisoned inside him.

"Your time is up, daughter. I will use your bloody limb and tear this house apart until I find *The* Heart of the Cat," he vowed.

"No, *your* time is up," Walkyr replied.

Trescina saw the weapon Raul was holding in his good hand. Her cat, already thirsting for revenge, tore through the fragile thread of her control. She released a guttural cry full of her grief and fear as she shape-shifted.

Her cat slammed into Raul. She locked her powerful jaws around the wrist of his remaining arm and bit down. He swung out at her with his metal arm, smashing his fist against the side of her head. Pain exploded through her, but she refused to release her grip until he dropped his weapon. His next blow caught her in the side, breaking several of her ribs and knocking the breath out of her.

Her body went limp when he grabbed her by the nape and flung her through the air. She would have landed in the other room if Walkyr had not wrapped his arms around her. She cried out when his hold tightened around her broken ribs.

"Pallu, kill him," Walkyr shouted.

Trescina turned her head into Walkyr's chest when she heard the sound of laser fire. She closed her eyes. Behind her, she heard the unexpected sound of glass shattering followed by a heavy thud. Raul's harsh curse was cut short.

She turned her head when she heard Pallu shout out a warning. Walkyr pulled her through the doorway he had entered through and sank down against the wall with her in his arms. She struggled to shape-shift, ignoring Walkyr's harsh warning to remain in her cat form.

"Ah," she cried as her broken ribs shifted.

"You shouldn't have changed," he growled in frustration.

Her head fell back against his arm. "Who is shooting?" she moaned.

"It has to be a human. We do not use such weapons," Walkyr stated, looking over at his brother where he had taken refuge.

"Cinnamon and Spice," she fretted, looking up at him.

"They are safe. They are in the garage," he softly reassured her.

"Pallu, see if you can discover who is behind this," he said.

Trescina saw Pallu give a brief nod before he disappeared through the door leading to the garage. She tucked her face against Walkyr again. It hurt to breathe. She moaned when he gently lifted her in his arms, turned, and strode down the hallway to her bedroom.

He carefully laid her on the bed. She lifted a hand to her throbbing temple even as she tried to cushion her ribs with the other. Walkyr pulled the small device he had used to heal his leg from the utility belt at his waist.

"This is much better than the barbaric medicine of your world," he said with a reassuring smile, gently pressing his fingers against her bruised neck.

Trescina nodded and closed her eyes. She could feel the soft touch of his fingers as he tenderly tilted her head toward him. A moment later, a feeling of warmth swept through her. Almost immediately the pain faded.

She opened her eyes and looked up at him. "I was going to run," she confessed, her eyes darkening with the emotion swirling through her.

"I saw that. Did you forget to tell me something?" he inquired with a hint of accusing sarcasm.

"Maybe. I didn't know you well enough to share that I'm a shape-shifter. We haven't even been on a first date yet," she retorted with a shrug before she winced in pain. "Ouch, that hurts."

"What is a date?" he asked.

She relaxed as the scanner began to work its magic on her broken ribs. Her eyes drooped. She didn't know if it was because she had gotten very little sleep in the past three days, had an emotional and physical crash from the stress, or from the warmth of the medical device; but her eyelids were getting heavy.

"I'm crashing," she murmured with a slight slur.

His warm chuckle sent a wave of calm through her. "It is the sedative patch I gave you. You should wake up in about five hours or so," he teased.

"You're a regular… comedian. Who knew they had those in…. space? Guess it is better than a knife to my throat," she joked in a barely audible voice before she sighed and gave up the fight against unconsciousness.

The last thing she remembered was the tender caress of his fingers across her temple. "No, no knives, Princess. Only a man who can't wait to take you on your first date—once I ask Riley or Tina what that is," he replied.

A small smile unknowingly curved her lips, and her cat sighed with contentment.

This better than running, her cat finally admitted.

CHAPTER TWENTY

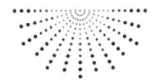

Three weeks later:

Big Cypress Reservation, Florida

Trescina looked up from where she was wiping down the last of the cabinets in the fifth wheel that she was donating to a pair of love-struck stargazers who had been married forever—aka Willie and Nora.

"I can't believe you are just giving us your truck and camper, Trescina. Are you sure we can't pay you for it?" Nora asked, standing up from where she had been storing some of the canned goods for their next trip.

Trescina looked at Nora and shook her head. "No, trust me, I can't take it where I'll be moving. I'd rather give it to you and Willie," she said with a smile.

Nora looked at her. "We didn't do any kinky stuff in here if that is what you are afraid of," she teased in response.

Trescina blushed. She had thought more and more about the 'kinky stuff' over the last three weeks. It didn't help that her cat was pushing her to get over her reservations and just do it.

"I'm not worried about it if you did. It's your camper now. I just don't want to think about whether I've wiped over any spots where Willie may have had his bare ass," she retorted.

"What is that about my bare ass? Nora, are you bragging about me again?" Willie called from the door.

Nora rolled her eyes and chuckled. "Only on the number of mosquito bites you can take," she hollered back.

Trescina listened with amusement as Nora and Willie flirted. She lifted her gaze to the window. Walkyr was standing outside talking to Willie and Nora's son, Thomas, and Ron, Thomas' friend. Her gaze softened when she saw him bend down to affectionately scratch Thomas' dog on the head.

"Where are the tigers? It seems strange to see you without them," Nora commented after Willie left to rejoin the men.

"They are enjoying their new temporary home," she murmured, still watching Walkyr.

Nora came to stand next to her. "Where did you meet him? He's a bit odd, but I like him," she said.

Trescina chuckled. "We met by accident. He was searching for something called *The* Heart of the Cat and he found me instead," she confessed.

"Well, I'd say that he found what he was looking for all along then," Nora replied. Trescina leaned against Nora when the older woman wrapped an arm around her waist. "I forgot the new towels I purchased. They are in the truck. I'll be right back."

Trescina absently nodded. She reached up and pulled the chain of her necklace out. She played with the red gem. She furrowed her brow as she thought about what Nora just said.

I'd say that he found what he was looking for all along then...

Trescina parted her lips on a soft gasp. Of course! She excitedly lifted the chain off of her neck and looked at the gem again. This time, she really *looked* at it.

Turning it over in her palm, she saw that the gem had a slight crack. She rubbed her finger across the line. She blinked in surprise when a section of the gem opened to reveal electronic components. This wasn't a precious jewel or a gem containing some magical power, it was man-made.

"It is a tracking device," a woman's voice behind her said.

Trescina gasped and turned. She stumbled backwards when she saw the ethereal woman made of gold standing in the middle of her fifth wheel. She took another step back when the woman looked curiously around her.

"I have never been in one of these. It is… interesting," the woman murmured.

"Who… who are you?" Trescina choked out.

The woman's expression softened. "I am Aikaterina. I gave your mother that device," she said.

Trescina shook her head in confusion. "Why? They… The Sarafin think it is the source of all their power," she said.

Aikaterina touched the device in her hand. "But you know the truth," she murmured.

"It isn't a stone. It is our own heart and the connection we have with our cat. It can only be taken away if we imprison ourselves with fear, hatred, or through our blindness and greed," Trescina shared and then she frowned. "But then…why…?" she asked.

Aikaterina took the stone in Trescina's hand and placed the necklace back over her head. "You will make a truly beautiful queen for your people, and Walkyr will be a strong mate to have by your side," she said, gently touching Trescina's hair.

Trescina narrowed her eyes and bit her lip. "What about Katarina? I'm trying to find her. I want her to come with me," she said.

A mysterious smile curved Aikaterina's lips. "Your sister has her own destiny to follow," she replied.

"Mason is here. He asked if you are ready to leave," Walkyr called from the door.

Trescina turned to look over her shoulder. "Yes, just a min…," she started to say before her voice faded. She was alone once again. She lifted her fingers to the necklace again and smiled. "Yes, I'm ready," she answered.

∼

Six months later:

Orbit of Sarafin

A soft moan slipped from Walkyr's lips. Trescina giggled and lightly ran her fingers over the bare skin of his chest. She leaned over him and pressed a kiss to one swollen nipple. He moaned again.

"I know you're awake," she said.

Walkyr's lips twitched, and he opened his eyes enough to peer down at her where she was lying with her chin on his chest. She grinned at him. It was hard to believe that they had been together for only six months.

"I like it when you wake me up," he teased.

She lifted her head. "No, you like getting up," she retorted, sliding her hand down his stomach and hip before moving it ever so slowly toward the hard evidence that he was fully awake and aroused.

Trescina squealed when he suddenly moved, gripping her arm and rolling her over onto her back so he could cover her with his muscular frame. Over the last six months they had done a *lot* of kink in this bed—and in the bathroom and on the small dining table and the couch and over the back of the couch.

"You are aroused," he murmured, his lips leaving a burning trail of hot kisses against her skin.

"I'm thinking of when you bent me over the back of the couch," she breathlessly admitted.

This time the moan he released was much louder. Trescina's legs parted when he pushed his leg between them. She instinctively raised them to wrap around his waist.

"Oh, yes, it felt a lot like this, only deeper," she purred.

She lifted her hips when his bulbous head pushed against her. She knew what was going to happen, and just the thought made her wet and ready. She dug her nails into his skin and pressed her heels against his buttocks to drive him deeper into her welcoming core.

He rewarded her by thrusting deeper into her before pulling back and doing it again. Her cat went wild. Pulling him down on top of her, she bit his shoulder. She was immediately rewarded with another deep, intense thrust.

She could feel his cock thickening as his desire increased. Her body tightened. Teasing him awake had been enough foreplay to get her red-hot and aroused. She had noticed over the last week that just a look from him made her ready to find a secluded spot so that he could ease the ache inside her.

I in heat. It get much hotter, her cat happily informed her.

Now you tell me! she gasped as her body stiffened, and an intense orgasm spiraled through her.

"I will never get enough of you," he gritted out between his teeth as he rocked his hips in the primitive dance of claiming and being claimed. "Goddess, but I love you, Trescina."

"I love you, too. My cat's in heat," she confessed.

Her admission sent him over the edge. She felt his cock expand, stretching her. The heated wave of his hot cum as he pulsed inside her sent her cat's hormones into a frenzy. Her body immediately reacted, releasing a chemical that his cat responded to.

"Goddess! It will be a miracle if we ever make it out of this room," he groaned, pulling her close and holding her tight—his body still locked to hers.

"At least we won't have to worry about mosquitoes," she sighed, sliding her hands down and massaging his buttocks. "Would you like to try the shower next?"

EPILOGUE

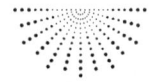

One month later: Forest Kingdom on Sarafin

"I can't believe heat can last that long. How can anyone get anything done? I mean, can you imagine if I was like that every month? It would be non-stop fu—," Trescina said before her words were cut off by Walkyr's mouth. She looked up at him with a dazed grin as he stepped back. "Why did you do that?"

"Because if you don't stop talking about the different ways we can, did, or should make love, I swear we'll never find the Forest Kingdom," he confessed.

"Maybe we should have brought Cinnamon and Spice with us. They are always a good distraction," she reflected, turning to walk along the path again. "Look! There it is."

Walkyr nodded. The golden orb was dancing just out of reach. Whenever Trescina's conversation turned to their love life, the orb would respectfully give them a little privacy. So far, Trescina's discussion had resulted in three detours and two baths in nearby rivers.

"Trescina," Walkyr quietly said, grasping her hand.

She glanced up at him before she turned in the direction he was staring. She parted her lips in awe. The mist had dissipated, and all around them, beautiful flowers were blooming. Trescina reached out and touched one.

Walkyr stood still when he saw several men and women approaching along the wide path they had been following. He recognized a few of them, including the two older warriors.

"Welcome home, my Queen. I am Trevine, the Captain of the Guard to your grandparents," Trevine greeted.

Trescina's eyes shimmered with tears when she saw the scars of battle on the old warrior's face. She stepped forward and reached for his hand. Squeezing it, she looked around at the warriors silently waiting to greet her.

"Hello. My name is Trescina Bukov-d'Rojah. This is my mate, Prince Walkyr d'Rojah," she quietly greeted.

Walkyr nodded to Trevine, and watched as Trescina met each warrior halfway. She listened intently to their greetings and repeated their names. The warriors were like the flowers of the forest feeling the warmth of the sun after centuries without its touch. Not only did hope return to the forest people, but so did their Queen.

∼

Several nights later, Trescina stood looking out over the kingdom. She had been hesitant at first, unsure of what to expect from the people who lived here and whether or not they would accept her. Her fears had quickly been extinguished thanks to the unconditional and heartfelt acceptance of the residents. Trevine and the other people of the kingdom had greeted her with open arms. She and Walkyr had briefly returned to the ship to gather clothing and the two Siberian tigers. That respite had given her time to adjust to everything she had learned.

Now, she contentedly listened to the sounds of laughter and music as it drifted through the air. She looked up at the night sky. A soft sigh escaped her as she gazed up at the stars and thought about how much her life had changed in such a short period of time.

"Are you alright?" Walkyr quietly asked coming up to stand behind her.

She released another sigh, this time one of pleasure when she felt his hands slide around her waist. She leaned back against his hard body. A small smile curved her lips when she realized that he had removed his shirt. Her hand slipped down and back. The smile on her face grew when her hand encountered bare flesh.

"Did you forget something?" she teased.

He softly chuckled and pressed a kiss to her neck. "It is easy to do when I see you," he admitted.

"I love you, Walkyr," she murmured, tilting her head back to look up at him.

His arms tightened around her. She didn't miss the pleasure in his searching eyes or the way he continued to search her face. She knew he had been worried about her when they left Earth. It was hard to miss with the attentive way he hovered over her. Of course, the way the other warriors on the warship had treated her with a deference and almost reverence had been a little weird, too.

"What are you thinking about?" Walkyr murmured.

She looked back out over the kingdom. "Everything," she quietly said with a shake of her head. "This is so... I don't know, overwhelming. There is so much I don't know or understand. Why did power mean more to my father than my mother's love—and me? Today I met so many wonderful but wounded souls. People who loved my grandparents and my mother. So many lost loved ones, and yet…." She stopped speaking when intense emotion from what she had heard, seen, and felt washed through her.

"The people of the forest knew as long as the Heart of the Cat was safe, there was hope, and that one day their Queen would return," he said.

"It should have been my mom," she replied. "A part of me wishes that she was still alive, so she could see this again, but another part of me knows that she never wanted to come back. She had found happiness on Earth with my step-father."

"I would have liked to have met her and your step-father," he murmured.

"Ivan would have loved it here," she said.

It was true, her step-father would have embraced a life here with her mother whereas her biological father had betrayed the very thing that he was. She had not argued when Walkyr had quietly suggested that Raul's body be taken back to the warship—to conceal any evidence of their presence, he'd said, but she thought it was really to give her closure. Raul may have been a horrible person, but he was still her biological father. The recessive memories of her cat gave her a vivid knowledge of the love her mother had once had for the man.

Whoever had killed him hadn't yet been located. Pallu and Mason had returned several hours after the attack. They had found imprints in the snow that indicated the attacker was a man. Pallu's cat had followed his tracks back to a road, but they had arrived too late. There was no definitive proof, but she suspected that she had been the target—not Raul. She had confessed as much to Walkyr and the other men.

"Have you heard whether Pallu has found Airabus yet?" she wondered.

"No, nothing yet. Airabus had moved the ship. The trackers that Qadir had attached to the ship had been removed. Pallu says he is working on a different method to track it. If anyone can find Airabus, it is Pallu," he assured her.

"I think the only thing I truly regret is not being able to speak with Katarina before I left," she confessed in a wistful tone.

"Chad swore he would find her and tell her what happened. If she wishes to come to our world, she will have safe passage," he said.

She didn't reply. Her heart ached for her younger sister. They had been so careful about keeping their distance in order to protect each other.

Trescina's only hope was that whoever had been searching for her over the years would not know about Katarina. Her sister had been born in their Russian home. Her father had said that their mother was terrified that a doctor or hospital would discover that she was different. The only documentation for Katarina had come from the falsified identification cards her father had purchased from an old friend who worked in the government. Even during the assault, Katarina had remained hidden near the river—unseen by their attacker who had escaped.

Walkyr tenderly turned her in his arms and lifted his hands to cup her cheeks. She could feel his concern for herself, and she gave him a wry smile. She ran one of her hands along his chest while her other hand dipped down below his waist. Her fingers wrapped around his growing length. A thrill of delight ran through her when she felt the rumble of a purr slip from him.

"I'm okay, really," she promised with a wicked smile.

"Run with me," he encouraged, bending to press a soft kiss to the corner of her mouth. "My cat wants his mate. He has been clawing at me since we set foot on the planet. I think he is done waiting."

"Show me," she breathed, turning her mouth to capture his lips.

Excitement swept through her. Their time on board had been filled with learning about each other. Her cat had been impatient to mate with his, but Trescina had been wary of releasing her cat when there were so many men surrounding them in the cramped ship.

"Follow me," he quietly instructed.

He pressed a hard kiss to her lips before stepping away from her. Her eyes glowed with pleasure as she watched him shape-shift into his leopard. A giggle escaped her when Cinnamon jerked up her head from where she was sleeping in the room. Spice jumped down off the bed and trotted out the door to sniff him.

Trescina giggled again when Walkyr turned and swatted at Spice with an expression of disgust and indignation. She stepped forward and knelt between the two large male cats. Spice purred, flopped down, and rolled over to have his belly rubbed.

"You are such a big, jealous baby. You still aren't used to not being the only furry guy in my life, are you?" she teased.

Spice rolled until all four of his paws were in the air. Shaking her head at the big goofball, she chuckled when Walkyr impatiently nudged her arm. She gave Spice one last good rub before she turned to look into Walkyr's beautiful eyes.

"Spice, stay with your sister," she softly ordered.

You finally stop being mean? her inner cat huffed.

Patience makes the heart grow fonder, she retorted.

Patience make me hornier, her cat replied.

Trescina chuckled and focused. She felt the familiar tingle as her body changed. The ancient blood of her ancestors ran through her body, and the power of it thrummed through her more intensely than she'd ever felt it before.

We home, her cat purred.

Trescina couldn't have picked a better way of describing it. They were home. There was no longer any need to be afraid that someone would discover she was different.

She released a long, deep, rumbling purr and rubbed her body down the length of his before curling her tail around his muzzle. A wave of warmth swept through her when she heard his aroused growl. Brushing against his hindquarters, she repeated the action on his other side. This time when she reached his neck she nipped him.

You are going to get us well and truly in deep trouble with this little tease, she warned her cat.

He got to catch me first, her cat gleefully retorted.

In a blink of an eye, her cat took off along the balcony. She leaped gracefully up onto the railing before jumping down onto a thick branch; the sound of Walkyr's aroused snarl echoing behind her.

∽

Walkyr's cat was beyond ready to take his mate. He was struggling to keep his grip on the beast. He had been doing well until Trescina decided to play seductress. His neck throbbed from where she had nipped him. If he hadn't been lost in imagining all the different ways he wanted to take her, he wouldn't have been startled when she suddenly took off.

Chase! his cat snarled.

Yes, we chase, Walkyr agreed with a devilish grin.

His cat took off across the balcony, and bounded through the trees, following the blue striped black tiger as she led him away from the palace and deep into the forest. Calls of encouragement from nearby women and laughter from nearby men spurred him on.

He didn't know if it was instinct guiding her or luck, but they soon came to a small grassy meadow. He paused on a limb of a tree as she jumped to the ground. Her glossy black coat glistened in the moonlight as she trotted through the tall grass to a stream.

He landed on the ground and followed the trail she had cut through the grass. When he was couple of yards from her, he crouched and waited. She was taking a deep drink from the stream. He watched as she lifted her head and turned, searching for him. He slowly circled behind her. Her tail swished back and forth as if beckoning to him.

He struck when she turned her head to look behind her. His large cat covered her body. He sank his teeth into her neck and wrapped his front paws around her chest. Her startled hiss quickly changed to a deep purr. He felt her hips rise and her tail move to the side.

Together forever, my beautiful mate, he murmured as he slowly sank into her.

Forever, Walkyr, Trescina cried out.

∼

Several hours later, Walkyr held Trescina's soft, warm body in his arms. They had returned to the palace after giving their cats time to learn and explore each other. He would not be surprised if this became a nightly event—he certainly wouldn't complain if it did.

He ran his hand along Trescina's bare skin when she sighed in her sleep. A cool, light breeze fluttered through the open doors. The only sounds now were those of the night and the occasional snore from either Spice or Cinnamon.

A sense of peace settled over him as he continued to gently caress Trescina. He realized that she was right about the Heart of the Cat. All this time they had believed that the Heart was a gem, but it was actually a symbol that offered a reflection of who they truly were. Without understanding who they were, they could forget that their cat is a part of them, not a creature to be dominated and suppressed. Raul and those that followed the teachings of the *Enlightenment* had not been the only ones confused by the meaning of the scroll. He and his brothers had also been mistaken.

He turned his head and pressed a kiss to the top of Trescina's head. She was his Heart. He understood now what his brothers Vox and Viper had discovered—his true mate along with the heart of his cat and himself. Love was neither something to throw away nor something he would ever take for granted. He realized the emotion was also not something that was delicate and definitely not easy.

She delicate, his cat said with a wide, contented yawn.

She's precious, he corrected with a sigh.

A shudder ran through him when Trescina's hand slid across his stomach and moved down to grip him. His fatigue vanished as she began to stroke him. She tilted her head back and gave him a drowsy-eyed smile.

"I thought you were asleep," he murmured.

She rolled over on top of him, straddling his waist. "I was, but I had a dream," she said, looking down at him with eyes filled with desire.

"What kind of dream?" he asked.

"How about I show you?" she murmured, leaning down to press a kiss to the corner of his mouth.

Walkyr lifted his hips as she aligned his cock with her welcoming depths. His hands gripped her hips as she slowly impaled herself on his hard shaft. Their groans mixed with the sounds of the night. The two Siberian tigers lifted their heads. A moment later, they both rose to their feet and silently exited the room.

∼

Out on the balcony, Spice padded ahead while Cinnamon raised her head. Long, gold fingers scratched the white Siberian tiger affectionately behind the ear.

"It is good to have her home," Aikaterina murmured.

Trevine, the new Captain of the Guard, protectively stood watch from his position on the lower wall of the palace. The old warrior raised his scarred face when he saw two white tigers and one gold one playfully run along the thick branches of the tree before they disappeared into the night. His eyes followed them until he could no longer see them.

"Thank you, Goddess, for protecting the heart of our people," the old warrior murmured as a single tear coursed down his ravaged and withered cheek.

To be continued:
The Leopard and the Lioness

Pallu d'Rojah remained behind on Earth, searching for an alien traitor, but that isn't his only mission! Can he convince the stubborn single mom that aliens aren't as scary as she might think?

Coming soon.

Read on to discover other series!

River's Run
Lords of Kassis Book 1

River Knight was looking forward to a peaceful vacation in the mountains with her two best friends, Jo and Star, her fellow circus performers and sisters of the heart, but instead, River witnesses her friends' abduction! She silently follows, even going so far as to sneak aboard their spaceship. The rescue attempt doesn't happen fast enough though, and River finds herself on an unplanned vacation to the stars…

Check it out! books2read.com/Rivers-Run

The Dragon's Treasure
Book 1 of The Seven Kingdoms series

USA Today Bestseller!
A romance that revives hope when all seems lost.

Long ago, a strange entity came to the Seven Kingdoms to conquer and feed on their life force. It found a host, and she battled it within her body for centuries while destruction and devastation surrounded her. Our story begins when the end is near, a portal is opened, and a curvy klutz stumbles on the last dragon left alive….

Check out the full book here: books2read.com/thedragonstreasure

Touch of Frost
Magic, New Mexico Book 1
Sci-fi and Paranormal Fantasy collide!

When a maximum-security fugitive escapes to a distant, forbidden planet whose inhabitants have not mastered space travel yet, it's Star Ranger Frost who is sent after him.

Lacey Adams is a widow who owns an animal shelter in Magic, New Mexico, an *unusual* small town, to say the least, and she is certainly not easily taken hostage, not by the fugitive and not by the Star Ranger who wants her for himself.

Check out the full book here: books2read.com/Touch-of-Frost

ADDITIONAL BOOKS

If you loved this story by me (S.E. Smith) please leave a review! You can discover additional books at: http://sesmithfl.com and http://sesmithya.com or find your favorite way to keep in touch here: https://sesmithfl.com/contact-me/ Be sure to sign up for my newsletter to hear about new releases!

Recommended Reading Order Lists:

http://sesmithfl.com/reading-list-by-events/

http://sesmithfl.com/reading-list-by-series/

The Series

Science Fiction / Romance

Dragon Lords of Valdier Series

It all started with a king who crashed on Earth, desperately hurt. He inadvertently discovered a species that would save his own.

Curizan Warrior Series

The Curizans have a secret, kept even from their closest allies, but even they are not immune to the draw of a little known species from an isolated planet called Earth.

Marastin Dow Warriors Series

The Marastin Dow are reviled and feared for their ruthlessness, but not all want to live a life of murder. Some wait for just the right time to escape....

Sarafin Warriors Series

A hilariously ridiculous human family who happen to be quite formidable... and a secret hidden on Earth. The origin of the Sarafin species is more than it seems. Those cat-shifting aliens won't know what hit them!

Dragonlings of Valdier Novellas

The Valdier, Sarafin, and Curizan Lords had children who just cannot stop getting into trouble! There is nothing as cute or funny as magical, shapeshifting kids, and nothing as heartwarming as family.

Cosmos' Gateway Series

Cosmos created a portal between his lab and the warriors of Prime. Discover new worlds, new species, and outrageous adventures as secrets are unravelled and bridges are crossed.

The Alliance Series

When Earth received its first visitors from space, the planet was thrown into a panicked chaos. The Trivators came to bring Earth into the Alliance of Star Systems, but now they must take control to prevent the humans from destroying themselves. No one was prepared for how the humans will affect the Trivators, though, starting with a family of three sisters....

Lords of Kassis Series

It began with a random abduction and a stowaway, and yet, somehow, the Kassisans knew the humans were coming long before now. The fate of more than one world hangs in the balance, and time is not always linear....

Zion Warriors Series

Time travel, epic heroics, and love beyond measure. Sci-fi adventures with heart and soul, laughter, and awe-inspiring discovery...

Paranormal / Fantasy / Romance

Magic, New Mexico Series

Within New Mexico is a small town named Magic, an… unusual town, to say the least. With no beginning and no end, spanning genres, authors, and universes, hilarity and drama combine to keep you on the edge of your seat!

Spirit Pass Series

There is a physical connection between two times. Follow the stories of those who travel back and forth. These westerns are as wild as they come!

Second Chance Series

Stand-alone worlds featuring a woman who remembers her own death. Fiery and mysterious, these books will steal your heart.

More Than Human Series

Long ago there was a war on Earth between shifters and humans. Humans lost, and today they know they will become extinct if something is not done....

The Fairy Tale Series

A twist on your favorite fairy tales!

A Seven Kingdoms Tale

Long ago, a strange entity came to the Seven Kingdoms to conquer and feed on their life force. It found a host, and she battled it within her body for centuries while destruction and devastation surrounded her. Our story begins when the end is near, and a portal is opened....

Epic Science Fiction / Action Adventure

Project Gliese 581G Series

An international team leave Earth to investigate a mysterious object in our solar system that was clearly made by someone, someone who isn't from Earth. Discover new worlds and conflicts in a sci-fi adventure sure to become your favorite!

New Adult / Young Adult

Breaking Free Series

A journey that will challenge everything she has ever believed about herself as danger reveals itself in sudden, heart-stopping moments.

The Dust Series

Fragments of a comet hit Earth, and Dust wakes to discover the world as he knew it is gone. It isn't the only thing that has changed, though, so has Dust...

ABOUT THE AUTHOR

S.E. Smith is an *Internationally Acclaimed, Award-Winning, New York Times and USA TODAY Bestselling* author of science fiction, romance, fantasy, paranormal, and contemporary works for adults, young adults, and children. She enjoys writing a wide variety of genres that pull her readers into worlds that take them away.

Printed in Great Britain
by Amazon